Twisted in the Darkness: Bound by Shadows

By A.K. Neane

Trigger List:

This Book Contains (But Is Not Limited To):

-A consensual but deeply questionable kidnapping Dubious consent that takes a long, messy road to get clarified.

-BDSM so intense you may need a glass of water and a safe word just reading it.

-A charming psycho with a label maker, a leather collar, and a dream.

-Heavy religious trauma, shame, and the soul-crushing kind of guilt (don't worry, we unbutton all that real quick).

-One heroine's spiral from "I shouldn't like this" to "yes please, more".

-Power exchange, punishment, possessiveness, and the delightfully dangerous line between love and control.

-Long looks, longer leashes, and just enough aftercare to keep your conscience twitching.

-Food play, pussy worship, ass play, steamy showers, electro-stimulation, spankings, bondage, and... emotional dependency as foreplay.

-Trauma bonding... but with orgasms.

-Absolutely zero respect for the safe/sane/consensual rulebook (this is Risk-Aware Consensual Kink—or at least it tries to be).

Plot? Oh yeah. But you came for the collar, didn't you?

Find detailed trigger list in back of the book...

Dedication-

To all the good girls hiding from themselves to please the people they were taught to obey— and for those who wear the mask of control to survive.

Table of Contents

DOMINA

Prologue

The only light in the room emanated from the blue hue of my laptop screen, its soft glow illuminating my face. The computer rested on my lap as I lay in bed, leisurely sipping a glass of white wine. The ellipses blinked at the bottom of the chat thread as I scrolled through the latest messages from Marianne. She was this perfect young thing, and our connection had deepened over months of late-night chats, evolving into a complex dance of dark desires and emotional confessions. Our bond had grown as real and tangible as any face-to-face relationship could offer. Yet, I was conflicted, torn between remaining merely an online sanctuary for her and yearning for something more profound. I needed it to be real, and I knew she did too.

Domina: Present yourself, pet.

Marianne: Yes, Domina. I am here. How was your day?

Domina: Long and stifling, but now I'm ready to play. Are you, pet?

Marianne: Yes, Domina. I need to, as my day was also long.

Domina: Do you want to talk about it first, or shall we save it for after?

Marianne: After, please.

Domina: Very well. Strip and present your body by kneeling for me, pet.

Marianne: Yes, Domina. *(Click to download image)*

Domina: Good girl. You're so beautiful, and your curves are perfect. Now, spread your legs for me, pet.

Marianne is typing…

I took in her loose, shoulder-length golden brown hair and milky white skin, her plump curves and round belly. To me, she was perfect, her beautiful ample body was one I would love to have my wicked way with. Her eyes, a wonderful hazel, were full of warmth. Right now, a hint of more green peeked through them, revealing her excitement and nervousness.

As I waited for the next picture, I switched screens to the "Find a Friend" site, sifting through the information I had collected from all of Marianne's confessions. The quaint diner where she worked had given away her hometown, merely a couple of hours from my place. She had mentioned walking a few blocks to and from work because her mother believed the exercise would be good for her. That woman infuriated me to no end.

I had pinpointed her street by casually calling the diner and inquiring about her. The unwitting manager confirmed I was seeking Marianne Evans—the only Marianne that worked there. I hung up immediately after. This led me to find the Evans family on Baker Street. Marianne had shared that they attended New Hope Community Church twice weekly and that her parents were heavily involved. Indeed, they were, as their complete family details were plastered online through the church's directory.

A smug smile curled my lips as I began to compile a document with all of Marianne's details: her address, her family's home phone number, her work route, routine, church activities, even little tidbits about her like her favorite foods and pastimes—those little things that made her uniquely her.

I tried to suppress my growing obsession, but the thrill of knowing intimate details about someone exhilarated me, and she clearly needed me. Her parents couldn't see beyond their own desires and their reputation; they would practically sell her off to the highest bidder if given the chance. My anger surged, and I clenched my fist just as my laptop pinged with another delightful photo of her, of my little pet.

Marianne: As you wish, Domina. (Click to download image)

Domina: That's perfect. Stay just like that. You please me greatly when you follow my commands so beautifully. Now, turn on the webcam. Let me watch you.

I watched as the mode on the chat switched to video, and Marianne's nervous yet excited face appeared on the screen. I smiled and touched the cool glass of the monitor, wishing she could feel my caress through the device. Then, I typed.

Domina: Look at me, pet. I want to see your eyes while you obey.

Marianne lifted her gaze to meet mine through the camera, her breathing deepening as our connection intensified.

Domina: You are doing wonderfully. Now, touch yourself. Start at your neck, move slowly down. I want to see you explore your body the way I would if I were there.

She hesitated briefly before her hands moved to her neck, tracing the line down to her collarbone, then further down to her breasts. Her movements were tentative but grew in confidence. I bit my lower lip, my own hand reached between my thighs to find the growing pool of warmth there. I typed with one hand as the other rubbed in sweet circles.

Domina: That's it. Show me how much you want this, how much you need my guidance. Take special care to touch your nipples for me, pet.

"Yes, Domina." Her breathy whisper came across the speakers, stirring a thrill within me. I let out a small gasp as I watched her hands continue their journey, her touch becoming more assured as she followed my instructions, the sight clearly fueling both of our desires.

Domina: Now, pause. Keep your hands on your hips. I'm going to guide you through something new tonight. Are you ready to trust me, pet?

"Yes, Domina. I trust you." Her voice shook slightly, a soft, needy whimper escaping her that only grew my want—no, my need for her.

Domina: Good. Now, I want you to breathe deeply and focus on the sensation of your own touch. When you resume, you will not only follow my commands but also let your body lead you to what feels good. Let go. Allow yourself to feel everything fully.

As my breathing quickened and my hips undulated to my fingers' movements, a moan escaped me. The only thought in my mind was, I am going to make this beautiful little thing mine, all mine.

MARIANNE

Chapter 1

Dread filled my soul as the sound of my feet striking the rough concrete sidewalk echoed the frantic rhythm of my heart. I longed to find the strength, the courage, to overcome my crippling fears. But, I wasn't brave. I wasn't a risk-taker. I was too damn responsible.

I walked home from my shift at the diner, my arms weighed down by the groceries I'd picked up along the way. The sun had already sunk below the horizon, leaving the neighborhood cloaked in shadows. I quickened my pace, skirting the graffiti-covered walls and avoiding the singular mural that always made heat rise to my cheeks.

My shoulders throbbed with each step, the strain of the bags pulling at my muscles, but I knew my parents would expect fresh ingredients for dinner. A proper meal was non-negotiable in their eyes, no matter how late I got home from work. Disappointing them wasn't an option I could afford.

When I opened the front door, I heard the familiar murmur of my mother's voice. She was seated at the kitchen table, her Bible spread open beside the half-prepared salad. She looked up, her gaze lingering on my figure, and frowned. I shut the door carefully, hoping she wouldn't notice how exhausted I felt, but she always did.

"Put those down, Marianne," she said sharply, gesturing to the counter. "You're late. There's so much still to do."

I kept my mouth shut and lowered the bags onto the countertop, then made my way to the sink. As I washed my hands, I felt her gaze on my back, that critical silence daring me to defend myself from some perceived shortcoming. When I turned around, she sighed dramatically, shaking her head.

"You've been eating too many greasy meals at that diner," she declared, tapping her fingers against the worn cover of her Bible. "Your weight is getting out of hand. You must be presentable and pure for your future husband."

Her words stung. They always did. I tried to swallow the lump in my throat as I moved around her, opening cabinets, pulling out a cutting board and a knife. My father's voice spilled in from the living room where he was still listening to a sermon on TV.

"What's that verse, Ruth?" he called out to my mother. "The one about a virtuous wife?"

My mother's eyes brightened. "Proverbs 31," she replied, almost proudly. "A wife of noble character who can be found? She is worth far more than rubies."

I fought the urge to roll my eyes and instead forced my attention on the groceries. Carrots, celery, an onion, a hunk of beef. They needed to be chopped for the soup that was supposed to accompany the rolls I had made this morning and the salad my mother had put together. The repetitive motions of slicing and dicing usually calmed me, but tonight my nerves felt as raw as the meat in front of me. I felt that familiar wave of shame wash over me. The shame for my size, for my tired feet, for the small flickers of rebellion I sometimes let myself dream of.

I tried to immerse myself in the task, cutting the onions into small cubes, trimming the fat from the beef, ensuring the pieces were uniform. My fingers felt wooden on the knife as I blinked away tears that sprang more from emotion than the pungent onions.

"Don't forget to season properly," my mother scolded, glancing over her shoulder. "You know your father hates bland food."

"Yes, ma'am," I said quietly, placing the beef chunks into a pot and coating them with oil and salt. I turned on the burner then stirred the meat until it started to brown, adding the chopped vegetables soon after. The sizzle hissed in the air, mixing with the constant low hum of the television sermon.

As the steam rose, warming my face, my mind drifted to the future I wasn't allowed to have. A life of my own, far from this suffocating, overbearing household. But, the idea of actually leaving felt as unattainable as the simmering steam rising from the stove.

"I'm almost nineteen," I reminded myself. "I could leave… if I dared."

But I never dared, not when my mother and father needed me here, fixing dinner, cleaning the house, doing all the things a dutiful Christian daughter ought to do. I stirred the pot but all I could think about was the day I might finally be brave enough to walk out that front door for good.

My father shut off the TV, the living room going silent except for his footsteps on the worn carpet. I added broth to the pot, watching the liquid bubble and swirl around the chunks of meat and veggies.

"I'll finish up here," I said, trying to keep my voice steady. If I could just hold it together until dinner was done and they were satisfied, maybe I could slip away to my room and find a moment of peace.

When the soup was finally simmering on low, my father wandered into the kitchen to inspect my work, nodding once in approval before taking a seat at the table. Sighing inwardly, I pulled bowls from the cupboard, trying to ignore how my mother's disapproving gaze swept over my frame.

"Set the table," she commanded. "Then bring over the food."

I obliged, arranging the utensils and bowls precisely. My parents liked things neat. "Proper Christian order," as they called it. Every piece of cutlery had to be placed just so, every dish angled perfectly.

But, just as I reached for a ladle to serve the soup, my mother's sharp voice cut through the clatter. "The salad is for you," she announced, pointing to the green leaves in the large bowl beside her Bible. "You don't need any soup. You've eaten enough for one day, haven't you?"

I froze, my cheeks flushing. I opened my mouth but no words came. She was telling me, *ordering me* not to touch the soup I had just painstakingly prepared. I gripped the edge of the counter, steadying myself, feeling the dull ache of resentment stirring somewhere deep inside.

"Yes, ma'am," I finally managed, my stomach twisting in hunger and shame. It wasn't the first time she had restricted my meals like this, and it likely wouldn't be the last. All I could do was stare at the bubbling pot of soup, wishing I had the courage to say something more than a single obedient phrase.

DOMINA

Chapter 2

Nestled in a quiet suburb, my home served as both a sanctuary and a studio. The exterior's modern lines and expansive windows belied the controlled chaos of creativity that defined the interior. Here, I managed my freelance graphic design career, dealing with high-end clients whose demands were as intense as they were profitable. My dual monitors, a constant fixture on my sleek desk, flickered with the pulse of ongoing projects and looming deadlines. The juxtaposition of art and order defined my professional life, each project fueling my reputation and my financial independence.

The rest of my house mirrored this blend of aesthetics and functionality. Art pieces that I had collected from various travels adorned the walls, each telling a story of a place and a moment in time. However, the most personal space was in the basement, my playroom. Hidden from casual view, it was a realm where my other passions took shape. The space was equipped with furniture tailored to the nuanced needs of my more niche activities. Though, it had been sometime since I had used it, as lately my whole world seemed to be lived online.

The digital realm was both my workplace and my playground. As a freelance graphic designer in my thirties, I had carved out a niche for myself, managing high-end clients and lucrative contracts that demanded both creativity and discretion. My days were a blend of intense focus sessions punctuated by client calls and the steady hum of my email inbox filling up. Yet, despite the demands, I thrived in this chaos, each completed project fuelling my reputation and, in turn, my independence.

Graphic design was a world away from the darker, more intimate passions that occupied my evenings. The BDSM community had been my sanctuary for years, a place where I could explore the depths of control and surrender with like-minded individuals.

My journey into a kink lifestyle had started in my early twenties, though it had been a part of me as long as I could remember. My first curiosity started at local clubs, and events then grew into a respected role as a Domme. The transformation was gradual but deliberate, marked by learning, experiencing, and eventually leading. With the birth of the internet and the ease of creating worldwide connections, leaders began to create little spaces for our community, forums to connect. Those online forums became my hunting grounds for knowledge and connections, where I could explore identities and dynamics shielded by the safety of anonymity.

It was on one of these forums that I began seeking something more permanent than the casual scenes at clubs. It wasn't like I didn't enjoy the experience of a scene, or the thrill of cracking the code on someone new. However, I longed for a lasting connection with a sub whose emotional and physical submission I could cultivate over time.

My search was meticulous, filtering through profiles and posts until I stumbled upon her—Marianne. She was a newcomer to the scene whose virtual footprints on a BDSM forum page caught my attention. Her posts, filled with hesitance and a poignant longing for understanding, drew me in. Also, with her being new to the scene, unclaimed and untainted by previous Doms who might have pushed her too fast or too far.

I felt drawn to reach out and try to connect one on one with her and after that first message thread I knew she was what I was looking for. We began a nightly ritual of conversations that delved into the complexities of dominance and submission, boundaries, and exactly what this lifestyle could look like in a long term relationship.

At home, surrounded by the tools of my trade and the comforts of my design, I planned our interactions with meticulous care. I knew the value of patience and the importance of building trust, especially with someone as inexperienced and vulnerable as Marianne.

Through our chats, I learned about her life, her hidden desires, and the stifling constraints imposed by her upbringing. I guided her through discussions about limits, safety, and consent, all the while weaving in questions about her day-to-day life. She shared more than she realized, her words painting a vivid picture of a young woman stifled by parental expectations and a community that preached conformity.

Each chat deepened my understanding of her, and with it grew my determination. As each revelation confirmed my resolve to be more than a distant guide. I needed to bring her into my world, to show her a life where her desires weren't sources of shame, but paths to fulfillment.

I settled into the soft embrace of my office chair, the screens of my dual monitors casting a cool glow across the room. I leaned my chair back, sipping a glass of wine after a long day of creative exertions, and pondered the next steps.

My screensaver flicked to a slideshow of abstract art, a visual echo of the complexities and contradictions of my life. Marianne's face, though only seen through this digital window, felt as familiar as the art pieces I lived with. I was ready to make a move from guiding her in the shadows to leading her in the light. My home, my sanctuary, would soon become hers too, if all went as I hoped. The thought was both exhilarating and daunting, but I was prepared. After all, in both design and dominance, I relished turning the chaos of potential into the beauty of reality.

I pulled up the webpage for New Hope Community Church and double-checked the service times. I knew which one she would attend, and I needed to see her in person. She had never seen a picture of me; I had been cautious about that, revealing very little about myself while gathering as much information as I could about her. Unfair, perhaps, but that was the nature of our dynamic. I was the Domme in control, and she, unknowingly, was my prey.

MARIANNE

Chapter 3

I stepped through the wide glass doors of New Hope Community Church, my flats making light tapping sounds against the polished concrete floor. The stage lighting was already set, awash in bright blues and purples, and a keyboardist softly played the opening chords of a contemporary worship song. The foyer buzzed with chatter as greeters in matching polo shirts handed out bulletins and ushered people inside.

My mother clutched her Bible against her chest, pressing me forward. "Hurry," she hissed, as though missing even a second of the service was a sin. Her eyes darted around to see if anyone was watching us arrive so late. My father had already slipped into the main auditorium, claiming our usual seats near the front row.

I followed them, weaving through the crowd of parishioners in jeans, sneakers, and the occasional floral dress. The walls were painted a welcoming beige, adorned with banners that read, "Come as you are!" and "Loved, Chosen, Forgiven." Typically, the sight of cheery volunteers, bright lights, and a casual stage would calm me, even if the sermons themselves could feel suffocating. Today, though, an uneasy restlessness gnawed at me.

As I slipped into my seat, the band on stage ended their warm-up, launching into an upbeat worship song. Strobe-like lights flashed in time with the music, and a display on the large overhead screens showed the lyrics. My mother stood, singing along, but I couldn't concentrate, not even when the lead vocalist called everyone to join in.

That was when I saw her. At the far side of the room, leaning casually against a wall, she stood tall and curvy, her presence impossible to ignore. Even amid the swirl of bright lights and echoes of amplified guitars, she drew my attention. Her dress was simple—black and snug—but it highlighted her full, generous breasts and cinched waist in a way that seemed out of place in this polished evangelical space.

Her dark brown hair, cut in a short bob just above her shoulders, framed a face with warm brown eyes. She watched the crowd with a kind of composed detachment, neither swaying to the music nor clapping like the rest. Something about her stance was self-assured, almost like she was here on her own terms rather than out of religious obligation.

The pastor took the stage as the song ended, encouraging us to greet one another. My mother shook hands with a smiling couple in the next row while I looked again in her direction. That was when, just for a moment, our eyes locked. The faintest, knowing smile touched her lips, and my pulse kicked up as if responding to some silent command.

I tore my gaze away, attempting to focus on the pastor's words as he welcomed newcomers and prayed over the offering. Still, I was painfully aware of her presence across the room. I chanced another glance; she hadn't moved, but her gaze hadn't wavered either. A tremor ran through me, equal parts fear and curiosity, as though she could see every conflicted thought I harbored.

When the sermon began, lights dimmed around the auditorium, drawing all attention to the pastor on stage. I tried to listen, really I did, but I caught myself repeatedly turning my head, scanning the perimeter for her. Each time I looked, I found her eyes, that same unblinking, intent gaze. Heat crept across my cheeks as I forced my eyes forward, sinking a bit lower in my seat as if it could hide me.

The pastor's voice rose and fell, urging us to live righteously in a broken world. My mother's fervent "Amen" rang out along with the others in the audience, but none of it registered in my mind. My heart pounded like an offbeat drum, attuned only to that mysterious woman who seemed so confident, so vividly at odds with this place's polished earnestness.

When the band returned for a closing worship set, I hastily tucked my purse under my arm and excused myself from the row, pretending I needed the restroom. My parents glanced at me disapprovingly but said nothing. Heart thudding, I pushed through the people in the aisle, searching for her—yet by the time I reached the doorway, she was gone.

I stood there in the hallway of the church, feeling the dull buzz of the fluorescent lights overhead, the muffled bass of the worship music still echoing in the auditorium. The air smelled faintly of coffee from the church café. A few latecomers hurried past, but she was nowhere in sight. My chest felt strangely hollow, as though I had lost something precious without fully realizing I possessed it to begin with.

Even as I returned to my seat beside my mother, anxiety twisted in my stomach. I couldn't forget the way that woman's gaze had pinned me in place, nor the soft curve of her lips that hinted at a secret only she and I shared. A million questions crowded my thoughts, each more unnerving than the last. Who was she? Why did she look at me like that? How did she command the space around her so easily?

I sang the closing song on autopilot, voice barely above a whisper. If anyone noticed my distraction, they said nothing. Yet I carried the haunting imprint of that stranger with me as we filed out of the auditorium with the rest of the congregation. For a moment, I allowed myself to dream of what it would feel like to step into the world on my own terms, not my parents', not the church's, and to stand as confidently as she had in a place that had always felt so stifling.

DOMINA

Chapter 4

I slipped through the wide glass doors of New Hope Community Church, my presence barely noticeable amidst the buzz of the congregation. The foyer was alive with the soft hum of conversation as volunteers in matching polos distributed bulletins with practiced smiles. The polished concrete floor reflected the stage lights, casting vibrant hues of blues and purples around the room, while the soft chords of a contemporary worship song played in the background.

From my discreet vantage point near the entrance, I scanned the crowd, noting the casual attire of jeans and sneakers mixed with the occasional floral dress. The walls, painted a soothing beige, were adorned with banners proclaiming messages of acceptance and forgiveness. It was a setting designed to comfort and welcome, yet beneath the surface, I sensed the same stifling conformity that Marianne had described.

I caught sight of her almost immediately. She was a beacon of unease in the flow of parishioners, her mother close at her side, clutching a Bible tightly against her chest and urging her daughter forward with a harsh whisper. It was clear that arriving even a moment late was a grave concern. Her father had already claimed their seats near the front, marking their territory in the social hierarchy of the congregation.

Marianne moved with a hesitance that tugged at my resolve, her expression one of resigned compliance as she navigated through the crowd. The cheerful volunteers and the church's vibrant atmosphere did little to mask the restlessness that seemed to gnaw at her, a stark contrast to the environment that was meant to offer solace.

As they disappeared into the main auditorium, I lingered towards the back on one side and leaned against the wall, observing quietly as the music started. I crossed my arms over my chest, my sleek black dress simple and unassuming. I aimed to be forgettable among these people.

Then, I noticed her gaze flicker to mine. She had seen me. A surge of possessiveness welled up inside me. I wanted to snatch her up and kiss her right here, in front of everyone, to prove that their rules and tales of hellfire were nothing more than silly stories meant to frighten the weak.

She stood singing, alongside her parents while slowly swaying, her figure easily distinguishable by her loose, shoulder-length brown hair and the modest dress that seemed a size too small, clinging awkwardly to her curves. The dress, likely chosen by her mother, covered her sufficiently but couldn't disguise the fullness of her form. Her parents, standing rigidly on either side of her, occasionally offered sharp whispers and stern looks, correcting her posture or her engagement with the service.

As the music faded and the congregation began greeting each other, I stood firmly in place. Our eyes locked again, and I let a smirk play across my lips, confident she could feel the intensity between us. It was evident in the subtle shift of her posture as she took me in. I knew that if I could touch her at that moment, she would be wet and ready, her body visibly responding to our invisible connection. As the crowd settled, the pastor began his sermon.

As the pastor delivered his sermon on the virtues of obedience and purity, I watched her closely. Her expressions shifted subtly, a mixture of resignation and distance clouding her features. It was clear she was performing the motions, her participation mechanical, devoid of the fervor that animated the faces around her.

Her mother's hand occasionally reached over to adjust Marianne's hair or smooth the fabric of her dress, each touch seeming more corrective than affectionate. Her father, meanwhile, sat stoic and disapproving, his eyes rarely meeting hers, instead focused forward, absorbed in the sermon or perhaps in his own appearance of devoutness.

The service dragged on, and with each passing moment, my resolve hardened. Seeing her in this environment—the suppression, the control, the expectation to conform—clarified everything for me. Marianne didn't belong here, confined by invisible chains forged by her parents' stringent expectations. She deserved freedom, a chance to explore who she could be away from all this.

I decided I wouldn't approach her today. No, today was for watching, for confirming the truths hidden in her messages—those little confessions she typed with trembling fingers late into the night. I needed to understand the depth of what she endured, to witness firsthand the life she needed rescuing from.

As the congregation began to disperse, I lingered for a moment, watching her interact—or, more accurately, not interact—with the other churchgoers. Her parents were quick to usher her out, barely allowing her time to exchange more than a few hurried pleasantries.

I followed at a distance as they walked to their car, a modest sedan that looked as stern and unyielding as her father. Once they drove off, I made my way back to my car, parked a few blocks away to avoid any unnecessary attention. As I sat behind the wheel, the image of her, trapped in that life, that dress, that family, fueled a fierce protectiveness within me.

I turned the key in the ignition, my mind racing and my emotions high. I would save her, not because she was a damsel in distress—no, Marianne was more than that. She was a flame smothered by the oppressive hands of her parents. And I? I would be the oxygen that would allow her to burn bright again.

I left the church with a plan forming in my mind, the pieces falling into place with a clarity that both excited and daunted me. She needed someone who could appreciate her fully, who could challenge her and cherish her. She needed me, not just as a Domme, but as a savior from the life she was too scared to leave behind on her own. The drive home was filled with a mix of anticipation and purpose, my thoughts already on how I would bridge the gap from the digital shadows to her tangible reality.

MARIANNE

Chapter 5

I stood behind the counter of the diner, the fluorescent lights glaring off the chrome coffee machines. My wavy, mid-length dirty golden brown hair was pulled back in a ponytail, and I tugged self-consciously at the hem of my uniform blouse. It fit poorly over my curves—too tight across my chest, crept up at my waist—just another reminder of how I never seemed to meet anyone's expectations, including my own.

Yet, despite the usual discomfort that gnawed at me, I couldn't stop replaying the memory of that woman in church. Every time I closed my eyes, I saw her gaze fixed on me, daring me to step outside everything I'd been taught was holy and correct. My heart tripped over itself, caught between fear and an unexpected spark of longing I'd never quite felt before.

I carefully refilled the napkin dispensers, trying to keep my hands busy and my thoughts away from the sinful flood of images: the curve of her hips, the confident tilt of her chin, the warmth in her dark eyes. A man at the counter called out for more coffee and I jumped. The pot rattled in my grasp as I hurried over to top off his mug.

"Thanks, sweetheart," he said. I forced a polite smile, but my mind was miles away.

I could hear my mother's voice reverberating in my head: *Purity is everything. A woman must guard her heart, her mind, and her body.* She had repeated that mantra as long as I could remember, but it took on a punishing tone when I first voiced something that went against the family's beliefs. I couldn't have been more than six years old. I stood in the living room, declaring loudly to my parents that I wanted to have a wife someday—and that I would be the husband.

I remembered how my father's face twisted in horror, how my mother's eyes blazed with indignation. My father grabbed me by the arm, marched me to my bedroom, and bent me over his knee. The spanking that followed was swift and humiliating, each strike accompanied by my mother's insistent voice telling me I was sinful, confused, an offense to God. Then they made me kneel by the foot of my bed, tears and shame burning my cheeks, reciting scripture I could barely pronounce.

"Jude 1:7," my father demanded, slamming the Bible in front of me. My small voice quivered as I read the words about Sodom and Gomorrah, every syllable driven by fear. Then came *Genesis 2:24, "Therefore a man shall leave his father and mother and be joined to his wife, and they shall become one flesh."* I stumbled through it, each word hammered in by the sting of punishment, each verse a searing reminder that, in their eyes, my thoughts were unnatural and vile.

I never forgot how that felt—how long the bruises ached, how the shame lingered. Even now, as I poured coffee for a smiling customer, part of me trembled under the weight of those memories, the echo of leather on skin and the sound of my parents' condemnation.

That memory always lingered at the edges of my mind, an ugly reminder of how wrong I was in their eyes. Sometimes, I convinced myself it was just a child's misunderstanding. But, ever since I started chatting in that forum with others like me, and then there was Domina, I had found a small space to lock it all away. A place outside of my daily life, an escape. However, seeing that woman at church, *whoever she was*, touched a part of me I thought I'd successfully buried. My worlds seemed to collide in that moment, and I wondered if Domina looked like her. Every time I pictured her calm confidence and the almost playful curve of her lips, my cheeks grew hot.

My mind kept drifting back to her. The mysterious woman's confidence at the church felt like a key turning in a lock. At times, I convinced myself that Domina was a man hiding behind a female persona to ease my guilt about all I had divulged. The thought of being drawn to another woman always made my chest tense, yet a flicker of warmth—of possibility—kept pulsing through me. I bit my lip and busied myself by wiping down the countertop, but my reflection in the shiny metal made my stomach twist. I tried to focus on my task instead of the rush of heat coursing through my veins.

Growing up, I was taught to believe my destiny was to become some godly man's wife, bearing children in obedient service to the Lord. And until that silent exchange in church, I told myself I'd eventually stop pretending online and make peace with that fate. Yet now, I found myself hungry for something outside the confines of devotion and duty. Something I'd been forbidden to want, let alone imagine.

My mother's warnings replayed in my mind like a relentless loop: Women were meant to be wives and bear children. Anything else, especially lustful thoughts about another woman, was unnatural. "An abomination," she would say. However, I couldn't suppress these feelings. The exhilaration that surged through me at church yesterday still vibrated within, pulsing with every heartbeat. It felt more real and intense than even the moments when I obeyed Domina, touching myself or showing her my body.

I glanced at my reflection in the polished metal of the coffee machine. My cheeks were flushed, and I couldn't decide if it was from the heat of the diner or the tangle of emotions I was trying so hard to bury. A little voice inside me, a voice I'd repressed for years, whispered that maybe what my parents claimed was sinful might also be what made me feel truly alive.

Shaking off the lingering tremors of memory, I offered a tight smile as I served a slice of pie to a waiting customer. But, no matter how I tried, I couldn't silence the storm inside. That equal mix of dread and exhilaration, a tug-of-war between my deeply ingrained beliefs and the undeniable pull I felt whenever I remembered her eyes on me.

My heart pounded. I wanted to dismiss that feeling, to attribute it to a moment's insanity. But the more I tried to suppress it, the more intensely it gripped me. After that silent exchange in church, everything felt altered. Could it be because of the things Domina and I had explored under the dim light of my bedroom during the late-night hours? Had it awakened something within me that was dark and possibly evil? No, the rightness of the relief and freedom I felt couldn't be denied. Something deep within me ached for more, regardless of how forbidden it might be.

I didn't know who she was. I had no idea if I would ever see her again. Yet, my thoughts refused to calm, swirling with questions. Questions I knew would only be safe to ask on the laptop screen at home, in that little chat box with Domina. I pushed aside my doubts for the moment and mustered a polite smile for the next customer. But, the biggest question lingered, *what if, for once, I truly followed my desire, dared to want something beyond their prescribed plan for my life?*

DOMINA

Chapter 6

As I paced the length of my bedroom, the floorboards creaked underfoot, mirroring the restless energy that surged through me. Scattered across the bed were the detailed plans of the operation, each step meticulously noted, each action calculated with precision. Tonight wasn't just about desire, it was about liberation.

Marianne's confessions during our last chat replayed in my mind, a haunting echo of her despair. She had divulged her parents' latest scheme to me. They had made an arrangement with an older Christian man from her church, someone the pastor had eagerly endorsed. They planned to try and marry her off to him. The very thought ignited a fierce anger within me. She didn't want this life. She needed an escape but saw no feasible way to break free on her own.

Sitting at my desk, I reviewed the final details of the plan. Abduction was a strong word, legally perilous, but what I was about to do felt more like an extraction. I was set to rescue her from a future she hadn't chosen and a life she dreaded. My preparations were comprehensive—everything from the route I would take to the timing that would ensure minimal exposure.

The essentials were already packed in my car: bindings, blindfolds, and other necessary items, all discreetly arranged. I had studied her daily routines, memorized her most vulnerable moments, and pinpointed the perfect time for our departure.

It would happen tonight, after her evening shift at the diner, as she made her usual stop at the alley to admire the provocative street art. That mural of women entwined in a loving embrace, a scene that seemed to captivate and comfort her. Despite the forecasted rain, I knew she would still pause there; it was a moment of solace in her otherwise oppressive life.

The laptop on my desk pinged with a new message from her, perhaps a prelude to our pivotal meeting tonight. She would be expecting a simple conversation, perhaps a comforting word or two. Little did she know, tonight was the night her life would change forever.

Marianne: I am about to leave for work but wanted to check in first, Domina.

I smiled softly, formulating the question that had been burning inside me.

Domina: You are such a good girl for me, pet. But... I have a quick question. Don't think too hard, just answer me. If you could be swept away from your current life and taken to a safe place, would you want that?

I held my breath as I watched the word *Typing...* flash on the chat screen.

Marianne: Yes... with all my heart.

I reassured myself of the necessity of my actions. Marianne had expressed feelings of being trapped, a fear of confronting her parents, and an inability to reject the life they imposed upon her. Her messages painted a picture of a young woman on the brink, yearning for a freedom she felt she could never grasp on her own.

I stood, looking at myself in the mirror. Reflected back was a woman determined, a Dominant ready to claim her submissive— not out of malice, but out of a deep-seated need to liberate her. Marianne's trust in me was complete, and with every exchange, she had unknowingly given me the keys to her shackles.

This was it. I would offer her a choice, a chance to take the control she never had. As I turned off the light and headed towards the door, the weight of my decision pressed down on me, not as a burden, but as a solemn duty. Tonight, I would liberate her, and show her exactly how much she could feel.

I got into my car and started the two-hour drive, my heart racing. I mentally checked off all my preparations. I would have to keep her, train her to feel free. Captivity for the purpose of freedom was not the most straightforward tactic, but I couldn't risk her simply going right back home. She needed love, affection, care, and I was prepared to give her that and so much more.

I had prepared a room just for her. Even though it was also my playroom, I had made it more comfortable for her stay. It was soundproof and secure, designed to let her undergo the process of detoxing from the brainwashing and trauma she had experienced.

As I drove through the evening traffic, my mind replayed every interaction, every confession she had shared. It wasn't just about the physical space I had prepared; it was about the psychological space I needed to create for her. In the end, I knew she would choose me and thank me for it. I knew our story could have a happily ever after.

The rain started to patter against the windshield, a rhythmic sound that seemed in sync with my increasing pulse. I turned on the wipers, their motion steady and reassuring. The weather report had predicted a downpour, perfect for a discreet operation. Fewer people would be out, and the sounds of the city would be muffled by the rain.

I checked the rearview mirror, ensuring I wasn't being followed. An old habit from a less savory part of my past, but useful tonight. As the city's lights blurred by, my thoughts shifted to the exact moment I would see her. She often lingered near the mural on 5th and Logan, a spot she'd described once during our chats. The street art that was a beacon for her hidden desires.

41

Pulling into a nearby parking lot, I shut off the engine and sat back, organizing my thoughts. The plan was straightforward: I'd present myself as a concerned acquaintance, someone familiar yet non-threatening. Given the rainy weather, I'd offer her a ride home, leveraging the casual kindness expected of a stranger in poor weather. In my coat pocket, I carried a taser, and the pouch that held prefilled injections of ketamine, just in case.

From that moment on, I would bring her home and to the place I had carefully prepared, equipped with everything needed to ensure her safety and comfort. Tonight, Marianne would finally be freed from her gilded cage, and I would be the one turning the key. The responsibility weighed heavily on me, yet my resolve was firm.

I glanced at the clock and it was almost time. Drawing a deep breath, I remained seated, watching intently for her arrival. Tonight, everything was set to change.

MARIANNE

Chapter 7

I dashed through the dark, rain-soaked streets, every cold drop amplifying the heat coiling inside me. My thin cotton shirt clung uncomfortably to my skin, making each inhale sharper and more urgent. To my right, towering buildings with rough brick and windowless walls loomed like silent sentinels, while to the left, an unkempt road stretched off into the distance. This was my usual route to and from work at the diner, leading me back to the cramped apartment I shared with my parents, my perpetual prison, or so it felt.

Yet tonight, the relentless downpour and swirling darkness didn't deter me. In fact, they lent me a strange sense of purpose, of daring. I paused at a particular corner, where a provocative mural adorned the brick wall, half-hidden by shadows and the glow of a distant streetlamp. Its lines and curves depicted a woman's figure, but in my mind, it blurred into a far more explicit scene: a woman bound in ecstasy as another woman kissed her bare breasts. The imagery jolted my senses, feeding fantasies I had only recently let myself imagine again. Especially after seeing her at church.

Rainwater dripped from my loose curls, pooling on my cheeks and trickling down my neck. I raised my fingers to the mural, tracing the painted curves as forbidden thoughts raced through my head. What would it feel like to touch a real woman? The question made my pulse spike. My mind immediately conjured that mysterious, confident stranger. My stomach flipped at the memory of her dark eyes meeting mine, of the silent command in her gaze.

Leaning my back against the cold, abrasive wall, I sank to the bare concrete. Rain seeped through my clothes, but I no longer cared. In this private, waterlogged sanctuary, I felt free in ways I never did at home—free from my parents' crushing expectations, from the weight of my own doubts and guilt. Closing my eyes, I breathed out the same silent prayer I muttered every night: to be rescued from the life I was trapped in, from the world that insisted on shaping me into someone I wasn't sure I wanted to be.

A sudden flash of bright headlights cut through the darkness, breaking my moment of solitude. A car, nearly silent against the backdrop of the storm, pulled to a stop not far from where I sat. My shirt, soaked and clinging to my body, offered no protection against whoever might be stepping out. Squinting, I tried to see past the glaring beams. A tall, curvaceous figure emerged, moving with quiet confidence.

My breath caught in my throat, and my heart pounded so loudly I feared she could hear it. It was her, the woman I had seen at church, who had since haunted my restless dreams. She advanced swiftly, every step hinting at coiled strength, like a predator honing in on its prey. I wanted to jump up and flee, but my body refused to move, rooted by a twisted sense of anticipation and terror.

"Can I... help you? Do you need directions?" I asked, my voice coming out in a trembling rush. I felt utterly exposed, my back to the wall, the rain sliding over my skin. A wave of regret slammed into me—I should have run the instant I saw her silhouette.

She closed the distance without a word, standing mere inches from me. Rain glistened on her milk-white skin, flecked with a faint bronze glow, and her dark bob framed those deep brown eyes. Her gaze slid over me like a searchlight, taking in every quiver, every shallow breath. A cold shock of awareness prickled across my limbs, and I knew I was in far deeper waters than I'd ever ventured before.

Lightning seemed to charge the air between us. Her lips curved into a smile, one that made my stomach lurch in both fear and longing. I opened my mouth to speak, but the words never formed.

A sudden, twisting pain gripped my arm and throughout my body, fiery and immediate. I felt heavy and rigid all at once. I fell into her and she kissed my cheek and whispered something as a sharp pain pierced my neck. My vision swam, and a deep, enveloping blackness rushed forward before I could even scream.

Then everything went dark.

DOMINA

Chapter 8

Lightning cracked overhead, echoing the rapid pounding of my heart. Through the torrential rain, I spotted Marianne slowly walking, the sight of her skin tight wet clothes clinging to her curves only fueled my need to touch her even more. She paused at the mural, the same spot she said she would, and as my resolve hardened, now was my chance. Now was the moment. I licked my dry lips, convincing myself I was rescuing her from a life of misery. This time it will be different; it will end in my happily ever after-no, in *our* happily ever after.

I revved the engine and drove toward her, flicking the headlights to illuminate her figure and slowly pulling to a stop. Thunder clapped loudly as I stepped out. My hands threatened to shake as I approached her. She shivered, slightly trembling, like the prey she was, igniting a thrill of desire within me.

Should I ask her to let me give her a ride? No, if I do that she will know too much, overthink too much. If she thinks about this I know she will choose to go back to the hell that she calls home, the only place she knows. I have to take her completely, I have to…

"Can I... help you? Do you need directions?" Her voice, trembling like a sweet melody against the backdrop of the rain, filled the space between us.

I closed the distance until only inches remained, and she backed against the wet bricks. I took in her full figure, looking her up and down. I wanted to touch her, taste her, to claim her, make her mine in every way. I smiled and raised my hand, holding the taser to her arm. Before she could react, I pressed the button, and she slumped into my arms muscles tight.

"You're safe now, pet. You're all mine," I whispered, brushing her cheek with a kiss as I depressed the prefilled syringe of ketamine into her neck. Her body slackened almost instantly.

I carried her to the car and laid her gently in the back seat. The street was deserted, there were no headlights, no footsteps, and no witnesses.

As I drove, the city lights faded behind me. She would stay under as long as I kept the doses on schedule. I'd planned to stop to inject her again before we made it home.

I did it.

Now came the task of teaching her to love herself, to accept who she is, and to realize she is neither wrong nor bad. Glancing in the rearview mirror, I watched her peaceful face, framed by disheveled hair. Even in the dim light, she was breathtakingly beautiful.

Driving through the rain-slicked streets, the only sounds were the steady swish of the windshield wipers and Marianne's soft breathing in the back seat. Each breath she took seemed to synchronize with the beating of my heart, a constant reminder of the gravity of what I had just done.

As the car hummed along, my mind raced with plans and possibilities. The road ahead was not just physical but fraught with moral complexities I had yet to fully untangle. I had crossed a line tonight, one there was no going back from. The weight of my actions pressed down on me, but the thought of Marianne, trapped in a life she didn't choose, bolstered my resolve.

Turning onto the highway, the city lights blurred into streaks of color through the rain. My grip on the steering wheel tightened as I considered the depth of the deception, the abduction, and its intended salvation. How would she react upon waking? Fear? Anger? Resignation? I had to be ready for all of it.

As the miles ticked away, I rehearsed what I would say to her, how I would explain that this drastic action was born out of necessity, out of a desire to give her the freedom she longed for, but was too afraid to seize on her own.

The room I had prepared was both a sanctuary and a cell, tailored to nurture and to hold. It was equipped with everything she might need to feel comfortable and safe as she adjusted to her new reality. Books that would intrigue her, music that would soothe her, and art that would inspire her—each chosen to reflect what I knew of her tastes and desires.

Pulling into the driveway of my secluded home, the finality of the evening's events settled in like the storm clouds overhead. I killed the engine and sat for a moment in the quiet, gathering my courage. I then exited the car and walked around to the back door.

Opening it gently, I leaned in and carefully unbuckled Marianne, lifting her once more. Her head rested against my shoulder, her body limp but safe in my arms. As I carried her inside, away from the rain and into the dimly lit hallway of my home, a mix of emotions surged through me: guilt for the method, but hope for the outcome.

"This is your new home, Marianne," I whispered, more to steady my own nerves than to inform her unconscious form. "Here, you will find yourself. Here, you can be free."

I crossed the threshold, the door closing behind us with a definitive thud, sealing away the world and beginning a new chapter that would test us both in ways I could only begin to imagine.

I carried her down the stairs to the basement, to what was both a dungeon and a playroom, but now it would serve as a sanctuary where she would discover love and care. I laid her gently on the plush bed, methodically removing her wet clothes with nothing but soft, careful caresses along her damp, cool skin. She was mesmerizing—every dimple, every scar, every freckle captivated me. I stretched her body out gently on the bed. Each wrist I secured into leather cuffs that were attached to chains at each corner of the bed. It was crucial to ensure she wouldn't harm herself or me. I would free her soon enough.

Next, I secured the leather cuffs around each ankle, and then she was perfectly exposed, spread out on the bed. My breath caught at the sight, a forbidden thrill rushing through me. I took the quilt and tucked it tightly around her naked form, ensuring she was warm and covered. Before leaving, I kissed her forehead gently, my hands trembling with the gravity of what I had done.

I walked out and headed to my own bed, locking the door behind me. As I slipped the key around my neck, a complex mix of emotions surged through me. She was mine now, and soon, she would understand that too. This room, meant for play and exploration, would now be her place of awakening.

MARIANNE

Chapter 9

I slowly stirred, waking to filtered sunlight warming my face, bright against the back of my eyelids. For a moment, my body felt weightless, as though I were floating on a cloud. Then, the pounding in my head began. I blinked, squinting at the light, my temples throbbing with each heartbeat. Instinctively, I raised a hand to rub the ache away and block the sun. A jarring clank of metal against metal stopped me cold, cutting through the fuzz in my mind.

Confusion prickled at the edges of my awareness. *Metal? What is around my wrist?* Alarmed, I tried to lift my other hand. Another clink echoed and I swallowed hard, my throat painfully dry. Why the hell was I chained to a bed?

Fear twisted in my gut, and my heart hammered, but I forced myself to take a measured breath. I glanced up at the stiff leather cuff around my wrist, which was attached to a thick chain leading to the iron bedpost. The same was true of my other hand, and the faint jingle of metal informed me my ankles were similarly restrained. Everything felt surreal, like I was stuck in a dream I couldn't wake up from. Though, the throb in my head and the dryness in my mouth were all too real.

My vision adjusted to the space around me. It was large, open, and completely unfamiliar—nothing like my cramped apartment. The décor exuded a dark elegance: crimson wallpaper with black lacy patterns and a tall, black ceiling supported by wooden and metal beams. A few lamps, placed strategically around the room, cast warm light. It felt both inviting and foreboding. The small, high windows allowed only a glimpse of the sky, offering no sense of time or escape. The furniture was strange, unlike anything I had ever seen, but each section of the space looked thoughtfully laid out. A single door, painted violently violet with black trim, stood furthest away from the bed.

I lay on my back against plush pillows that smelled faintly of lavender and sage. A thick cotton quilt covered most of my body, except for my outstretched arms. I tested the restraints again, and the unforgiving leather bit into my wrists. Panic threatened to unravel me, but a traitorous flicker of excitement lingered beneath it. *Did she bring me here?*

My mind raced, *I asked for this, didn't I?* I had prayed, every night, to be freed from my suffocating life. Not exactly this way— kidnapped, bound, and at the mercy of a stranger. But, I couldn't ignore the rush of heat pooling low in my belly. Some dark, hidden part of me thrilled at the thought of being utterly powerless.

I tried to move my legs, to pull them closer, but they were anchored to the opposite corners of the footboard. Anger, fear, and a strange longing warred within me. My throat burned, making it difficult to swallow. I was so thirsty.

A scream tore from my lips before I could stop it. "Help! Someone! Anyone! Let me go, please!" My voice cracked, echoing in the vast room. In the stillness that followed, I realized how futile it was. Nobody answered. Nobody came rushing to help. My parents weren't here to scold me for screaming, and the thought of their indifference dug under my skin. *How long will it take them to even notice I'm gone?* I let out a short, bitter laugh.

Suddenly, shame spiked. If they ever did find me like this, bound and trembling, *what would they say? That I brought it on myself? That I was sinful, unclean, asking for this kind of punishment?* And still, a relentless thrill snaked through me, whispering that this was what I'd always wanted, to be taken, claimed, seen in a way no one had bothered to look at me before.

I remembered admitting it to Domina in our chats more than once. Fuck, maybe this woman who took me was her. I had asked, no, begged, several times to see even a picture of her. She was always so careful, never revealing anything substantial about herself, while I laid everything bare before her, literally. The first time, well my first time ever, was only a couple of months ago when I finally got a webcam for my laptop, and I used it solely to strip off everything in front of it for her.

Just the thought sent a shiver through me and made me try to clench my thighs together to stop the liquid heat I knew was starting there. A throb bloomed inside me, I noticed a fullness I hadn't felt before but couldn't ignore and I squirmed, restless with need.

Time blurred, my hunger and thirst intensifying the headache behind my eyes. I must have dozed, because when I heard the scrape of a heavy deadbolt, my thoughts scattered. The door swung open, and I strained against the cuffs to see who entered. My pulse roared in my ears.

It was her, the tall, curvaceous woman from church, from the car, the one whose piercing gaze had been my last memory before everything went black. She stepped into the room with the same quiet assurance I remembered, her dark bob neatly framing her face, her brown eyes glinting with unspoken intent.

In that moment, every emotion I'd wrestled with—fear, anger, shame, forbidden curiosity—exploded, leaving me trembling against the mattress. My throat closed, words refused to form, and all I could think was one thing:

My God, what have I gotten myself into?

DOMINA

Chapter 10

I lay awake in my bed, my mind a whirlwind of emotions and plans. The silence of the house was deafening, punctuated only by my uneven breaths. I replayed the evening's events, the swift abduction, Marianne's unconscious form in my arms as I carried her to what I told myself would be a better life. The weight of my actions pressed down on me, a burden I was no stranger to, but this time, it felt different. It felt more *personal.*

I had done this before, yes, but always with someone I had met in person at a BDSM event or someone I had previously dated. There was a mutual understanding, a consent woven through the very fabric of those relationships, even when power dynamics skewed traditional norms.

This time, however, with Marianne, was different. Our relationship had blossomed in the shadowy corners of online chats, growing in intensity without ever crossing into the physical world until tonight. I had convinced myself that I was rescuing her, pulling her from the mire of a life she despised, yet the reality of my choice gnawed at me.

As the night stretched into the early hours of the morning, I battled with the confliction brought on by my choices. The difference this time was the screen that had separated us. The digital divide that somehow made the real world abduction feel more jarring, more *real.* Was I truly saving her, or was I imposing my will, crafting her into the narrative I believed was best? Yes, I had asked her, but was that truly consent? And, this time, did that even really matter to me?

I got up and paced the length of my bedroom, each step a thud against the hardwood floor. I thought about the others, the women who had come before Marianne. They had been part of the lifestyle, already initiated into the ebb and flow of dominance and submission. With them, there had been an immediate physical connection, an understanding and acknowledgment of what the relationship entailed from the outset.

Marianne was different. She was a canvas of innocence, painted with strokes of curiosity and a longing for escape. I had seen the potential for liberation within her, the desire to break free from her oppressive life. Yet, as dawn crept through the curtains, casting a pale light across the room, I questioned if my methods were just.

I had never forced anyone before Marianne. My previous experiences were mutual, consensual, even if they pushed boundaries. Now, as I prepared to face her in the morning light, I had to confront the possibility that I had stepped over a line from which there could be no return.

Sitting at the edge of my bed, I clasped my hands together, trying to steady the tremble. I knew what I had to do. I had to face her, to see if she would accept or reject the new world I had thrust upon her. The uncertainty was terrifying, but necessary. It was time to see if what I had done could truly be part of her salvation or if I had merely captured her under the guise of care, creating a new hell for her.

With a deep breath, I rose from the bed and made my way downstairs to the room that held more than just Marianne. It held the culmination of my desires and fears, intertwined in the delicate balance of power and responsibility.

As I descended the stairs, each step was laden with the ghosts of my past, each memory a reminder of the transient bonds I had formed. In the solitude of the predawn, my thoughts turned to those who had left, each departure a unique story of disillusionment and rejection.

Each relationship had started with a spark, a mutual attraction to the thrills and depths of a lifestyle that promised more than just conventional affection. They came to me as enthusiasts, eager and willing, drawn by the allure of relinquishing control, of exploring the shadows and nuances of their desires under my guidance. I was their Domme, their mentor, and for a while, their world.

But as the novelty waned, the reality of a sustained submissive lifestyle began to weigh heavily on them. It wasn't just about thrilling sessions or intense scenes; it was about the day-to-day dynamics, the psychological depth, and the emotional investments that such relationships demanded.

One by one, they confronted the permanence of what it meant to live under someone else's rule. They began to miss their autonomy, yearning for parts of their old lives that they had willingly set aside. The thrill of submission, once a liberating experience, slowly morphed into a burden for them. They wanted weekends of wild abandon, not a lifetime of structured obedience.

With each farewell, I felt a part of my own resolve crack. I questioned whether it was something lacking in me, a failure to fully encapsulate the nurturing yet commanding presence they initially sought. Each time, the pain of their departure was poignant, a sharp reminder of the delicate balance between dominance and the nurturing care I aimed to provide.

I realized that while I had been focusing on shaping them, I had neglected the crucial aspect of ensuring that this lifestyle was truly what they wanted for the long haul, not just a fleeting adventure. It forced me to reflect on my approach, to consider that perhaps my vision of a perfect submissive relationship was more about my own desires than a shared journey.

Now, with Marianne unconscious and lying vulnerable before me, I faced a crossroad. Her situation was a culmination of my desires to nurture and control, but also a mirror displaying my fears of eventual rejection. This time, however, there was no mutual starting point, no shared agreement to begin this journey, only my conviction that I was saving her from a life of misery.

I had to confront the possibility that what I saw as salvation, she might view as captivity. The fear that she too might leave, once she discovered the full scope of the lifestyle I had drawn her into, was paralyzing. But it was a fear I had to face, to truly understand if I had made the wrong choice.

As I stared at the door and unlocked it, I steeled myself for the confrontation to come. This time, I promised myself, I would listen more than I commanded. I would observe her reactions, gauge her true feelings, and see if there was a genuine desire within her to stay—or if, like the others, she would eventually seek to escape the world I had so carefully constructed.

MARIANNE

Chapter 11

She closed the door behind her, pulling a corded necklace
with a key from around her neck before locking the door with a
decisive click. I watched, my pulse quickening, as she placed the
necklace back over her head, the key now resting between her
large, full breasts. Her dark brown hair, swishing just above her
shoulders, accentuated her confident movements. She wore an
apricot-colored T-shirt with the words *"Grateful to be Blessed"* in a
cutesy design, and skin-tight black leggings that highlighted every
curve,exposing every crease.

For a moment, she lingered by the door, flashing me a warm
smile that sent a surge of apprehension through my stomach.
The moment stretched, tense and silent, until she turned and
crossed the room toward a small kitchenette in the corner. Bright
white counters spanned about eight feet, with neatly arranged
drawers and cupboards below. Next to the counter stood a silver
mini fridge, which she opened, revealing bottled water and an
assortment of cold foods.

She pulled out two bottles labeled *"Purified Water."* The word
"purified" triggered a distant memory: the pastor screaming in
my face, rancid olive oil dripping down my hairline, sermons of
rebuking evil and cleansing my soul of its "sinful" desires. My
parents had accused me of demon possession when a friend
claimed I kissed a girl, though I never really had the chance to.
Some friend she was.

When the mini fridge door thumped shut, I swallowed hard,
turning my attention back to the gorgeous older woman who
now approached the bed. She held the water bottles loosely
at her side, moving with predatory grace. My breath caught as
dread tightened my chest. *Would she kill me here?* The idea of
being alone, a virgin, nothing more than a token of my parents'
dedication to God, made my stomach clench.

I remembered my pastor preaching every couple of months, "Go forth, sons and daughters, bear fruit. Sons, cleave from your father and mother, take thee a wife, and multiply. The blessings of our God are in our children, the fruit of our loins, that they may continue in the work to which God has called us and lay claim to the earth." A chill ghosted over my spine and shivered at the thought of those words.

"Good morning, pet," she said softly, her voice soothing yet dangerous. My heart slammed against my ribcage. I couldn't tear my eyes away from hers. They were deep brown, brimming with a mix of mystery and something unmistakably playful, like a large cat toying with a trapped mouse. I opened my mouth to speak, but it was as dry as the desert. A feeble "Don't" rasped out.

She walked to the foot of the bed and bent down, checking something I couldn't quite see. I watched as her hand glided up from the floor, tracing the edge of the bed until it reached my leg. Then I felt it, her fingers following the line of something unfamiliar, running along my thigh and between them… and then inside me.

Heat rushed to my cheeks as she lifted the quilt to inspect me. Embarrassment prickled beneath my skin, but it tangled with a pulse of dark, coiled excitement in my stomach. A smirk curved on her lips as she murmured, more to herself than to me, "Looking all good."

"What is it?" I squeaked out, then winced as a painful cough racked my chest.

Her attention snapped to me and she tilted her head staring at me, feigning sympathy. "Poor pet, you must be thirsty." She lifted one of the bottles and took a long drink, the condensation sliding down over her fingers. Then she set the other bottle at her feet, letting out a contented sigh. "Would you like some, pet?"

66

I tugged fruitlessly at the cuffs locking my wrists to the bedposts, nodding with what little freedom I had. Her grin widened, and she pressed the open bottle to my lips. I gulped the water greedily, savoring the cool relief. But she tipped it higher, too high, and cold water flooded my mouth, spilling over my nose and chin, pooling at my chest. I gagged, coughing as the liquid stung my throat and filled my nose. I choked, unable to breathe. It was too much. I tried to jerk my head back, but it only filled me more with the water I craved. Painfully it burned down my throat and nose, pressing behind my ribs. *I can't breathe.* Just when I thought it wouldn't stop, my eyes bulged in panic until she finally pulled the bottle away and recapped it.

My lungs burned as I coughed and spit up the water, hacking desperately for breath. In that moment, any lingering confusion about our power dynamic disappeared. If it hadn't been apparent before, I understood now: she controlled everything, including whether I lived or died. And something about that was oddly comforting to me.

"Why did you take me?" I croaked once I found my voice, my throat still felt raw.

She reached out and stroked my cheek, her tone as gentle as her words were unsettling. "I couldn't very well leave a poor stray like you out there in the rain, could I? No. You needed a home, an owner." Her fingers brushed back strands of my damp ringlets, the simple gesture sending a shiver through me.

"Please," I pleaded, turning away from her intense gaze. "I already have a home… parents who need me."

Her hand caught my chin, forcing me to meet her eyes. "You need me, pet." The warmth of her breath brushed my lips, tinged with a lavender and citrus fragrance. My pulse hammered as she leaned in, her lips hovering just a hair's breadth from mine. Then, in one swift movement, her mouth claimed mine—urgent, demanding, and intoxicatingly sweet.

Her tongue parted my lips as a tremor of unexpected pleasure coursed through me. My heart thundered, drowning out all the guilty voices in my head. Her grip remained unyielding on my chin. I didn't fight it. *God forgive me*, I thought, even as a wave of heat fluttered through my lower belly. A slick desire, stronger than any I'd felt before, pulsed between my thighs.

She kissed me deeper, tasting of a sweetness that was both berry-like and faintly tart. I abandoned any thought of resisting, surrendering to the surge of longing that overwhelmed me. My body had never known such a potent need. Warmth rolled through my veins. My mind screamed that this was wrong, from everything I'd been taught told me so, but my body thrummed with a fierce, undeniable craving.

Eventually, she pulled away, just enough for me to see the satisfied smirk curving her lips. My breathing came in shallow gulps, my skin prickling with each pant. This was only the beginning. A fraction of what I'd fantasized about in the secrecy of my own thoughts, they were dark, forbidden visions I could never admit. But, now that her hands and mouth were on me, I couldn't deny how deeply I wanted it.

No one could stop this. Not my parents, not my preacher, not even me. She owned me, and for a fleeting, terrifying moment, I realized I wanted to be owned.

DOMINA

Chapter 12

I released her chin, my fingers lingering on her soft skin just long enough to send a shiver through her. The soft whimper that escaped her lips before she could catch it resonated deeply within me, stoking the fires of my desire.

"Oh, little pet, you don't want me to stop, do you?" I purred, my voice smooth and enticing as my finger trailed lazily down her neck, skimming the pool of water still clinging to her collarbone. Each touch was light, teasing, yet I knew it left a blazing trail of awareness on her skin. My hand moved lower, to the edge of the quilt tightly wrapped around her body, the only barrier keeping her from me.

Shivers rippled across her body, her nipples stiffening under the damp fabric. I inhaled deeply, the scent of her mingling with the sweet scent of lavender in the room. The mix of her vulnerability and desire was intoxicating.

"Please," she murmured, her voice a barely audible plea. It wasn't clear what she was begging for—freedom, release, or more of my intoxicating control. The wicked curve of my smile deepened as I felt her tension rise.

My fingers moved deliberately, sliding along her bare shoulder before gripping the edge of the quilt. With calculated slowness, I peeled it away, revealing her body beneath. The cool air made her skin prickle, and her sudden intake of breath filled the silence between us. Her cheeks flushed with heat as she pulled futilely against the restraints. The leather cuffs held firm, a reminder of her submission to my will.

I laughed, low and resonant, and it echoed softly in the room. It wasn't mocking but carried a dangerous amusement. I reveled in her struggles, my gaze roving over her exposed form as I memorized every curve, every line. Her full breasts, bared to the open air, rose and fell with each labored breath. The tremor that ran through her only widened my grin, my pleasure in her predicament palpable.

"Has anyone ever touched your soft, plush little body, pet?" I asked, my voice dripping with curiosity and command. Even though I knew the answer was no, because she'd told me so in one of our many chats. *Had she figured out who I was yet?*

My fingers traced the curve of one breast, then the other, exploring the landscape of her body as if I were the sculptor and she my creation. I moved closer to her sensitive peaks, circling slowly, deliberately, drawing out her anticipation.

She clenched her eyes shut, as if she was trying to block out the reality of this. Her chest heaved, and a scream tore from her throat that was raw and broken. The sound briefly filled the room before dissipating into the charged air. My heart felt stuck in my chest for a moment as fear briefly flooded me. Without another thought, I took charge.

I delivered a sharp slap to her cheek, her eyes snapping open, the sting painting her face with shock. My hand stung but the contact did what it needed to, grounding her to this moment, to this reality...to me.

"Completely unnecessary, pet," I admonished, my voice both scolding and teasing. "No one can hear you here. And while I do enjoy your screams, remember, you will only scream when I command it. Do you understand?"

She nodded, her expression a mix of fear and confusion. I softened my gaze, brushing my fingers across the reddened skin of her cheek, soothing the sting I had inflicted. Her face was so soft and warm.

My chest tightened with a complex tapestry of emotions— power, control, and an undeniable thrill. This was more than a game; it was a profound connection, a dance of dominance and submission where every gesture, every touch, was laden with meaning.

God, how I relished this. To be the orchestrator of her surrender, to push her boundaries and watch her struggle between resistance and desire. If she would only let herself go, and succumb to the depths of her hidden desires. I wanted nothing more than to watch this woman come undone by my hand.

I leaned in, my breath warm against her skin, my lips finding the tender flesh of her breast, craving more with each sweet and salty taste of her. I knew I wanted more. I teased her nipple with my tongue, drawing it into my mouth as a gasp escaped her lips. I moved my hands to steady her shaking form, my touch firm yet gentle, as I suckled and nibbled, coaxing her into the realm of pleasure mixed with pain.

I heard her breath hitch, and watched as she bit her lip, fighting the moans that threatened to spill forth. But the building heat in her core was undeniable. Her body betrayed her; her hips bucked slightly against the restraints, her flesh seeking relief. I grinned as I continued my teasing tasting of her.

Oh, the exquisite torture of it, the tight coil of pleasure unfurling within her, the heat on her skin, the pull of my mouth turning her nipple to a hardened point. This dance of pain and pleasure was my gift to her, a wicked salvation.

The sudden bite I delivered made her entire body shudder. I was tempted to succumb to the thrill of it, to the dark, to the delightful sensations that made my heart race and desire build deep in me. I could tell she relished the feeling, even as she fought it, her inner turmoil as palpable as the physical sensations clearly overwhelmed her. I suckled harder, turning her sensitive breast red under my lips.

73

"Oh, little pet," I murmured against her skin, my voice filled with satisfaction and dark promise. "You'll learn to love surrendering. That's the beauty of it."

I moved my hand lower, my fingers exploring the soft flesh of her stomach, trailing down to her thighs. Each touch sent an electric thrill through me, as if she was the forbidden thing I was touching. Her legs strained against the restraints, seeking escape yet finding none. She was completely at my mercy, and deep down that was everything I wanted and everything I knew she needed.

MARIANNE

Chapter 13

My chest tightened as a kaleidoscope of emotions swirled within me—fear, shame, and an undeniable flicker of something darker, something I couldn't name but couldn't ignore.

God, I wanted this so badly, to be forced to surrender, to indulge in all the wicked, sinful things I had dreamed of but could never admit, much less do. If I let it happen, if I fought just enough, then perhaps I could still be seen as only the victim, be blameless and maybe I could still cling to the illusion of innocence. Yes, I could fight her, not give in to the pleasure, the thrill of it, and just maybe I could still pretend this isn't what I would choose.

She leaned in, her warm breath ghosting over my skin, and her mouth found the curve of my breast. Her tongue flicked against the sensitive skin before she drew one nipple into her mouth. A gasp tore from me, unbidden and unstoppable. She held my breasts in place as they were so large they always flopped to the sides, her grip firm but gentle, as she suckled and teased, her teeth grazing just enough to make me squirm.

My breath hitched, and I bit my lip, desperate to stifle the sounds threatening to escape. But the heat building in my core was impossible to ignore. My body betrayed me, my hips bucking slightly against the restraints, seeking some kind of relief.

Oh, God, I loved this feeling. The tight coil of pleasure in my core, the heat on the sensitive skin of my nipple, the hard pull of her lips bringing the tip harder and to a point. *No, no, I can't give in. I have to just bear it, let her grow tired of me. But fuck, I would never grow tired of this.* She was a wicked demon sent to save me from my own personal hell.

The sudden sharp prick of her bite made my whole body shudder. I was tempted to ignore the sensation that thrilled me, that made my stomach flip and butterflies emerge in the most wicked and wonderful ways. I relished the feeling and bit my bottom lip harder, sucking it tightly into my mouth, closing my eyes amidst my muffled moans. I couldn't help but relish the pleasure it brought me.

"Oh, little pet," she murmured against my skin, her voice filled with satisfaction. "You'll learn to love surrendering. That's the beauty of it."

She moved lower, her fingers grazing the soft flesh of my stomach, trailing down to my thighs. Every touch sent sparks shooting through me, a maddening mix of anticipation and fear. My legs strained against the restraints, but there was no escape. I was completely at her mercy, and for the first time in my life, I wondered if that was exactly where I wanted to be.

Taking a deep, pained breath, I tried not to groan or moan; I could not let her win. But, her fingertips grazed the center of my universe, the most sensitive skin I had, to where I had never dared to let my hand wander, to touch myself on my own no matter how many temptations I had. No, a couple of times I had finally touched myself for the webcam for her, Domina, but never outside of that. Because, I was not strong enough to give into any of my own desires, my wants, my needs. They didn't matter.

There was no space for me to have those feelings, to feel those sensations; I was always there to care for every other person in my life. However, this woman, she wanted me. She wanted all of me and she was going to take it whether I was willing or not. I knew she was going to claim every part of me. Even the parts I thought were ugly and unworthy, every bit that I disliked and despised about myself. She was going to claim it as her own, and that made me hunger for her touch, need for the pleasure that she brought me.

Her fingertips tantalized in the liquid heat that dripped out of me, her fingers cool as she swirled them through my wetness and found the epicenter of my bliss, my clitoris. As she sucked harder on my nipple, a choked scream of pleasure escaped me.

I had never experienced such an immense sensation, such a quickening in my soul that I began to shake and shudder everywhere as tension tightened in my stomach, in my legs, and in my ass. Waves of climax pulsed through my spine, up my neck, and into my head.

I arched my back in electric, fine pulsing throes as I breathed heavily, rolling in ecstasy. The sounds I made I could not recognize as my own, and she relished in my response. She never let up, she never let me pause; she continued until she had gotten everything she deemed I could give her.

From that moment, I didn't care that my stomach had rolls of fat or that I could hardly see my feet past my boobs and stomach when I stood up straight. I didn't care that I wasn't the prettiest girl in the room or that the boys didn't notice me like they did all the other girls around me. I didn't care that all my parents viewed me as was a maid or a cook, someone to give them anything and everything they needed.

In that moment, I was nothing and I was everything to her, and she was everything to me, and I wanted more. I could no longer deny that I wanted to be hers forever, that I never wanted to feel the empty void of my loneliness again, that I never wanted to feel the incessant life-sucking need but to be desired, to desire and need something back. I wanted this.

Her gaze locked onto mine as she released her mouth from my nipple. With a wicked smile and a tender voice, she spoke. "You were perfect, pet. I'm done for now." Yet, she didn't remove her hand from between my legs, still dripping with my arousal. Her fingers danced in slow circles that brought throbbing fluttering waves through my core.

My breathing steadied, yet my hips matched her slow, deliberate movements, still needy and wanting. I looked into her eyes and saw her satisfied grin as she lay across my breasts, watching my every response. It felt comforting and intimate, a closeness I had long craved. I never wanted this moment to end.

DOMINA

Chapter 14

She was the perfect mix of wanton desire and palpable fear. She was a needy, conflicted, pleasure-starved, humiliated creature. She craved it all, more than she even knew. The shame, guilt, and humiliation was ingrained for her entire life over her primal needs made her the perfect submissive for someone like me.

I watched her body quiver from the aftershocks of the orgasm I had just gifted her and lifted my fingers, coated in her, to my lips. Her scent was addicting, and I flicked my tongue out, savoring the taste of her wet sweetness—a flavor I knew I would come to crave.

Her hazel eyes, now flecked with more amber, stared at my lips. I smirked as I licked my fingers clean of her, watching her suck her lower lip between her teeth. She wanted more, undeniably.

I leaned forward from my seat next to her on the bed and kissed her. Our lips met, my tongue exploring her whimpers of need. I wanted to make her come over and over again, but I would show her just how much her body irrefutably wanted me.

I tangled my fingers in her hair and continued to kiss her with abandon, pulling her head back slightly, firmly, to let go of her lips as she gasped. I traced the line of her jaw with my tongue.

"You want more, don't you, pet?" I whispered in a husky, heated voice. My breath turned heavy with my own desire, my tight leggings soaked. Soon enough, I would show her how to worship me in every sense of the word.

My hand, free of her hair, trailed down her side, fingers gliding along her hip bone and over the plush, soft skin there. I teased my fingers down the top of one thigh and up the top of the other, each touch feather-light, before my lips found her earlobe. I embraced it with my mouth, my tongue twisting into its crevices.

She let out small whines as she tugged at her restraints, struggling to clench her thighs together in an attempt to resist the new rising sensations. I kissed down her neck to her pulse point and sucked hard. She gasped, filling her lungs as she arched her back.

Sliding my hand between her thighs, I cupped her dripping cunt— firm but careful, mindful not to disturb the catheter I had placed while she was unconscious. Then I nipped at her neck, claiming her with a bite as possessive as it was intimate.

I was determined to bring her just to the edge and leave her there, craving more of me. The rush of warmth in my core, knowing I had complete control over her, was the only high I craved. Maybe that made me sick, or perhaps it made me twisted. All I knew was that this primal need of mine was not satisfied without it.

I sucked her pulse point harder and gripped her hair tighter, holding her firmly in place, entirely at my mercy. I raised my other hand an inch above her center and smacked down in a firm, quick movement, eliciting a sharp squeak from her at the shock of pain.

I grazed my teeth over the bruised flesh beneath my lips and delivered another quick smack to her sensitive pussy. She emitted another startled squeal, and I gently rubbed the tender, reddened skin, drawing a hissed moan through her clenched teeth. Watching her body writhe under me, her hips bucking to receive more of my touch, was hypnotic.

"Use your words, pet," I purred, my smile turning wicked as I watched her struggle with herself, her need for me taking over.

"Please," was the breathy whisper she finally let out.

"Please what, pet?" I smirked, my fingers playing lazily, tracing teasing circles along the outer edges of her hot, wet, swollen cunt.

"Please... fuck me, please, Domina." Her whisper was more of a confession than a request, revealing that she recognized exactly who I was, not just a stranger, not merely a predator, but her salvation, the lifeline she desperately craved.

I released her hair and caressed her cheek, smiling warmly as I slowly pushed a finger into the depths of her warm, soft, quivering need. I kissed her lips softly, sweetly, with tender care, capturing the deep groan that rumbled through her entire body with my mouth. She was all mine, and she desired it profoundly.

I pulled back, my finger moving slowly inside her wet depths, and held her gaze. "Not yet, pet," I murmured, slowly withdrawing my finger along her clit, then thrusting it back in just as slowly and deliberately.

She arched against me as I teased her clit with increasing pressure before thrusting my finger deeply back in, each whine and moan, every soft sound of her desire filling me with such delight and satisfaction that I knew my own pleasure was inextricably tied to hers. She owned me more than she even realized.

As her breathing grew more erratic, I intensified the rhythm, watching her struggle against the waves of pleasure I orchestrated. "You're doing so well, pet," I encouraged, my voice a low hum against the charged air between us.

Her eyes fluttered open and shut, a silent testament to the intensity of her sensations. I slowed my movements, deliberately drawing out the anticipation, my touch becoming a promise of more to come.

"Please, Domina, I need—" she gasped out and I placed a finger gently against her lips.

"Shh, patience." I whispered, my gaze locked onto hers, compelling her to feel every second of the wait. I removed my hand from her, resting it on her stomach, and she whimpered at the loss, her body tensing in expectation.

My other hand smoothed down her hair, sweeping a strand away from her face, as I savored the sight of her desperate, eager form. I decided to leave her like this, wanting and needing me, to give her time to truly think about this… About me.

MARIANNE

Chapter 15

I struggled to catch my breath, my gasps ragged and uneven. She sat there, watching me in the most loving way, her features softened in that moment. Her rich brown eyes roamed over me, taking in every detail.

After a moment, she brought her fingers to my lips, commanding in a seductive, honey-coated tone, "Lick them clean." Mesmerized by her and what she had done to me, I complied without complaint. Initially slow, I simply stuck out my tongue and licked just the tip of her finger.

Seeing my mouth part slightly, she took it as an invitation, pushing her fingers deeper into my mouth, forcing it wider. "Suck, pet," she commanded, and I did, wrapping my lips around her fingers and sucking my own essence off of her. The taste was a salty sweetness I hadn't expected to enjoy, and surprisingly, I wasn't disgusted; I just wanted more of her, more of this, and I would do anything for it, even though it scared me and made me question my sanity.

But I didn't have to worry about that, right? She was, after all, forcing me to do this. This wasn't really my choice after all, it wasn't my doing. I could relax, knowing I wasn't to blame. Despite this conflict inside me, I pushed it aside. I continued my task, sucking and licking her fingers clean, the saliva from my mouth dripping down my chin and cascading past my throat into my hair.

I didn't care. I wanted to please her, to make her proud, to make her as happy as she had made me. The thought of making her happy brought a joy to me that I had never known before.

"Good girl, pet," she whispered as she removed her fingers from my mouth. I wanted to taste more of her, all of her. I felt a desire for her that I had never experienced before.

But then, reality hit me hard. She had kidnapped me. I was naked and tied to a bed, and she was having her way with me. How messed up was that? *Jesus forgive me*, I thought, my mind reeling into a spiral of self-deprecation and shame, and I began to cry.

What was I doing? I thought amid tears. *Why did I crave such debauchery?* I was definitely going to hell for this, but it felt so good, and I wanted this. *Maybe I can convince her to let me go now,* the voice inside shaken by fear and unsettled anxiety.

"Are you going to let me go back home?" I barely asked, my voice cracking on the word 'home'. The tears dripped down my cheeks wet and cool. Her thumb wiped away one of the tears as her gentle caress soothed my heart.

She looked down at me, her lips curling into a smile. "Pet, you are home." A new wave of emotions: dread, relief, worry, concern, excitement, and joy washed over me. I was so conflicted, torn between my desires and what I thought was right.

She pulled the quilt back over me, tucking me in like a child, her movements deliberate and gentle. Leaning in close, she whispered softly, "I'll be back after a while. Try to get some rest; you'll need it."

I had no idea what she meant by that, but her words lingered in the air, heavy with unspoken intent. I shifted uncomfortably, my focus fixed on her as she turned away. Even as she moved, her presence remained, filling the room like a tangible force.

She reached the door, unlocking it with ease before slipping through. The sharp click of the lock echoed in my ears, sealing me in. I was alone with my thoughts, my fear, and the growing uncertainty of what would come next.

DOMINA

Chapter 16

I leaned against the now shut and locked door, sighing as I sank to the cool, hard floor. Resting my head against the door, I closed my eyes. My hands trembled as I placed them on my bent knees. She was crying, asking about home—that hell she called home. My jaw clenched, and a soft growl escaped me. A very real part of me wanted to kill her parents, so if she ever did leave me, she couldn't return to them; to the abuse. I took a deep, steadying breath. No, even I had my limits, and cold-blooded murder, I liked to believe, was beyond them.

I pushed off the floor, steadying my breathing as I stood. Moving away from the door, I began the routine tasks that grounded me—cleaning, organizing, preparing for my client meetings. As a freelance graphic designer, my days were filled with deadlines and demands, high-end clients requiring constant creativity and perfection. Yet today, my mind wandered constantly back to Marianne.

I booted up my computer, the screen lighting up as I pulled up the designs I needed to finalize. Normally, the work would consume me, the art and design providing a necessary distraction from the complexities of my personal life. Though, as I adjusted a color here, tweaked a layout there, Marianne's tear-streaked face haunted every moment. Her voice, her pleas, her undeniable fear mixed with a confusing blend of desire. It all echoed in the back of my mind.

I paused, my finger hovering over the mouse. *This isn't like the others,* I reminded myself. *She reached out to me first. She wanted an escape.* My doubt lingered, a nagging fear that perhaps this, too, would end like the other times. Each had left, one by one, deciding the lifestyle and the depth of submission I demanded were too much. They rejected the life I offered, a life I believed could free them just as I hoped to free Marianne.

Sipping my coffee, I gazed out the window. The sky was overcast, mirroring the turmoil inside me. I had always managed to keep a professional facade, but today it was cracking. What if Marianne decided the same? What if she, too, saw me not as a savior but as a captor?

I shook my head, dispelling the thoughts. No. Focus on the now. Focus on what you can control. I returned to my work, forcing myself to dive into the minutiae of graphic design, the lines and colors blurring into a form of meditation. Even as I worked, a part of my brain plotted, planned, and worried about the evening when I would return to the dungeon, to her. The thought was both a thrill and a terror. I needed her to want this life, to want me.

As the hours ticked by, I kept my hands busy, my mind occupied with tasks. The image of Marianne, the sound of her voice, the feel of her skin, it all pulled at me, drawing my thoughts back to the basement, back to the decision I had made to take her, to save her.

This had to work. It simply had to.

After hours of working, I finally took a break to do what I had been avoiding all day—checking on whether Marianne's parents had noticed her absence. My hands were steady as I navigated to the New Hope Community Church website, the place where her family was deeply entrenched.

Clicking through the site, I found the weekly bulletin, and there it was, a small note tucked between announcements for bake sales and bible studies: "Prayer Request for Marianne Evans, please pray for our dear sister to return to her home and the path of righteousness." The simplicity of the message, the lack of urgency, it irked me to my core.

I scoffed, a bitter laugh escaping my lips as I read the words again. *Return to the path of righteousness?* The hypocrisy of it all, the way they masked control under the guise of spiritual guidance, fueled a fire within me.

My heart hammered in my chest as anger coursed through me. They didn't understand, didn't see the cage they had built around her, calling it home. To them, she was just a stray sheep needing guidance back to the flock, not a person with her own desires and fears.

This confirmation only deepened my resolve. I was right to take her away, to try to give her a life free from that toxic environment. It was vindication, a sign that what I was doing was not just for my own desires but a genuine rescue.

I closed the browser with a sharp click, the screen going dark, reflecting my furrowed brow. I needed to see her, to reassure myself that I was doing the right thing. Rising from my desk, I made my way downstairs, my footsteps echoing slightly in the quiet of my home.

As I approached the locked door to the room where I had left her, my resolve hardened. Behind that door lay my chance to do something right, to prove that this time it would be different, that she wouldn't end up leaving like the others. This time, I could make her see that she was safe, that she was finally home.

With a deep breath, I unlocked the door and stepped inside. She was still asleep, her body peaceful beneath the blanket, chest rising slowly. I didn't want to wake her, but I checked her anyway, careful not to disturb the rhythm of her dreams. I picked up the small notebook where I'd been logging her vitals and time-stamped another entry. Pulse: steady. Fluid output: low. Liquid intake: still not enough. I tapped the pen against my lip, debating whether I'd need to run a saline IV. She hadn't been well-hydrated when I brought her here, but if I removed the catheter and gave her back some movement in the morning, she might catch up naturally. She just needed to drink more water.

95

I sighed and looked down at her sleeping form. Peaceful. Vulnerable. The bruise on her collarbone bloomed deep red and purple. A satisfied smile curled my lips. She was mine now—truly mine—and the possibilities unfolded before me like a banquet. Tomorrow, I'd make her favorite breakfast. She would eat well for me. She would recover for me. And then, she would surrender again.

MARIANNE

Chapter 17

After what felt like hours, though I couldn't be sure how long it really was, I fell into a deep, dreamless, peaceful sleep. It was the most refreshing sleep I'd had in a long time. When I woke, my mouth was parched, and the space around me was dark, with not a single light to be found. I drifted back to sleep, not knowing how long I slept—whether it was eight hours or twelve days. My stomach grumbled, hinting it had probably been a long awhile since I last ate.

The absence of clocks in this space was unnerving and spiked my anxiety. How long would it take before my parents noticed I was missing? Had they gone to the police? Was anyone looking for me?

What finally roused me fully was the click of the lock and the clink of high heels on the floor. I wasn't certain but I believed the elegant woman wearing them was Domina, the enigmatic woman I had met online. She called me "pet" which triggered a connection for me. If my memory served correctly, I had once asked her to save me, to take me away. A pang of hunger shot through my stomach, reminding me of its emptiness. Then, a scent wafted towards me, and I thought I smelled oatmeal and perhaps pancakes, the aroma of maple syrup warming the air.

She brought over a rolling cart table, the kind you see in hospitals or dental offices, sterile and metallic. She placed a bowl, which seemed to have utensils sticking out of it, onto the table along with a few other items. Then, she sat on a rolling stool and smiled at me. "Good morning, pet," she said cheerily. "Are we ready for some breakfast today?"

I nodded, my voice barely above a whisper as I replied, "Yes, please." Gathering a bit of courage, I hesitated before continuing, my nerves tingling with the weight of my next words. "May I ask you something?" I managed to say, my eyes searching hers for any sign of recognition.

She raised an eyebrow, a spark of curiosity lighting her features. "Of course, what is it?" she prompted, her tone encouraging yet measured.

Swallowing the lump in my throat, I took a deep breath, the air heavy with the sweet scent of maple which only seemed to underline the weight of my question. "Are you... are you Domina? The one from the chat?" My heart raced as I awaited her response, the simple question unleashing a torrent of possibilities.

She looked at me for a silent moment and smiled in a knowing way, but didn't answer my lingering question. Instead, she turned to the cart at her side as she sat on the bed next to me.

"Now, pet, with breakfast, you will get a bite of food for every good sound you make for me, do you understand?" she explained, though I looked confused.

"Ummm," I uttered nonsensically, unsure how to respond.

"It's quite simple," she continued, her voice steady and authoritative. "I have several instruments here, and I will use them on you. For every delectable sound of pleasure you make, you will receive a bite of food. However, if you scream, say 'no', or make any sound that I do not find pleasurable, you will not receive a bite of food. Instead, you will feel a stroke from this riding crop." As she spoke, she picked up a long black rod covered in leather, its tip fitted with a small square of leather. With a calculated motion, she slapped it against the palm of her hand, the loud smack making me flinch. "Have I made myself clear?"

"Uh, yes," I admitted nervously, still a bit unsure, but I grasped the basic concept of this game. It sent a shiver down my spine and knotted my stomach with both fear and excitement. Plus, the prospect of food made me happy, so I decided to play along.

She smacked my breast with the crop, just above the blanket. "The only appropriate response here is 'Yes, Domina.'"

Rushing to comply and eager to avoid another sting from the riding crop, I responded promptly, "Yes, Domina."

She removed the quilt, fully exposing my spread and naked body. A rush of heat filled me and wetness gathered between my thighs. She traced her hand down my stomach, her warm touch trailing lower. I bit my lower lip in anticipation.

Her fingers teased playfully along my slick thighs as they moved closer to where I ached for her touch. She observed me with the amused intensity of a cat toying with a mouse, a wicked smile lingering on her lips. I drew short, shallow breaths, my anticipation building until her fingers finally found my clit, tracing soft, sweeping circles. My breath hitched letting out a soft whimper, and I arched into her touch, my pussy eager for more.

"That's a good girl, my pet," Domina praised, placing a full spoonful of my favorite breakfast on my lips: creamy, buttery oatmeal laced with maple and brown sugar. I closed my mouth around the large bite, savoring the warmth and sweetness as much as I relished her touch.

She pulled on a pair of medical gloves and reached between my thighs. I flinched as she tugged on something inside me. The sensation was strange, slightly arousing, maybe, because I was so sensitive, though mostly it was just uncomfortable. It felt like she was forcing me to pee, even though I wasn't. I forgot myself.

"No, what are you—" Her sharp look shut me up instantly. That stern expression told me everything: I'd spoken out of turn, and I was in trouble.

101

She tugged again, and with a brief, sharp sting, I felt sudden relief. My body sagged against the bed. She held up a length of tubing, peeling away the tape that had held it to my leg with quick, practiced motions, like ripping off a Band-Aid.

I bit down on my lip hard, determined not to make a sound, even as it all clicked into place: why I hadn't needed to pee for however long I'd been restrained here. She had inserted a catheter. And now she was removing it.

I watched as she placed everything neatly on the bottom shelf of her metal cart. Then, she took a cold antiseptic wipe and began cleaning between my thighs. The sharp scent of alcohol hit my nose just before the sting followed, it was quick, clinical, impersonal. And yet, even this sterile touch made the heat inside me rise. I bit my lip, trying to stifle the moan that nearly escaped.

She smirked, just barely, but I saw it.

Next, I watched as she removed her gloves, then pulled out a small, acorn-shaped silicone device, coated it with something that looked like gel, and brought it between my legs, rubbing it up and down my ass crack. Fear and excitement bubbled up inside me, the uncertainty written on my face.

"Relax your ass muscles, by bearing down." she instructed. I tried, my legs shaking, as she pressed the odd-shaped device harder and harder against my asshole. The anticipation was exhilarating and painful. She pushed harder and finally, it slid into me. The sensation of fullness was overwhelming, and I let out a relieved breath and a pleasured moan at her inserting it into such a forbidden place.

"Good girl, you took that so well," she praised with wicked delight, then scooped another big bite of oatmeal onto the spoon and fed it to me. It was delicious, buttery, warm, and soothing. Maybe it was because I was so hungry, but it tasted amazing. I was grateful for the food and not a stroke from the riding crop.

I savored the bite, closed my eyes, and suddenly I felt a rumbling vibration in my ass that pulsed up through my pelvis. Oh God, it quickened my pulse in such a wicked way as I felt heat building in my core. "Jesus save me," I murmured, letting out another moan, and she grinned.

"Do you like that, pet?" Her fingers trailed up my slit as she watched me closely.

I whimpered, "Yes, Domina." She scooped another bite from the bowl and shoved it into my partially opened mouth. I choked a little on the food, yet I enjoyed the sensation of eating it.

However, I was too consumed with the vibrations flowing through my body. I was breathing hard, harder than was conducive to swallowing well, but I managed. I swallowed the bite, trying not to moan again because at that moment, I didn't want any more food. I wanted to cum. oh God, I wanted to cum so badly.

She grinned wickedly at me and moved her fingers through my wetness, then inserted one deep inside my throbbing pussy. It felt amazing, and I moaned loudly, "Fuck, that's… that's so good."

"Good little pet, cum for your Domina," she commanded as she shoved another bite of food into my mouth. I didn't know if I could handle it. I moaned loudly, and the oatmeal spilled from my mouth down onto my chest.

She smirked and removed her fingers from my throbbing cunt. "Uh-oh, looks like my pet has lost her food," she said as her fingers, soaked in my essence, smeared the oatmeal down my chest and across my nipples, which peaked at the sensation. She licked, lapping at the food, eating it off my breast, leaving behind a trail of warm wet stickiness that heightened the chill against my skin.

DOMINA

Chapter 18

The taste of her, intermingling with the sweet warmth of the maple oatmeal, only heightened my growing obsession with her, my need for her. Having her here—touching her, hearing her, smelling her, tasting her—ignited a primal urge within me to completely and thoroughly possess her, and I desired nothing more. Restraint was never my strong suit. Yet, this game of pushing her limits, training her, and showing her all that she desired but had always denied herself, was the thrill I craved.

I gently nipped her nipple, and the hum of the vibrating anal plug resonated through her, accentuating her soft, restrained moans. Smirking, I sat up and scooped another generous spoonful of oatmeal, guiding it to Marianne's lips.

As she swallowed the warm, creamy oatmeal, her eyes met mine, a mix of vulnerability and rising desire in their depths. I watched the subtle shift in her expression, a silent plea for more—more touch, more intensity, more of whatever I chose to give her.

"Enjoying your breakfast, pet?" I asked softly, my voice laced with an undeniable command. Her nod was hesitant but eager, a clear testament to the conflicting emotions swirling within her.

Leaning closer, I traced a finger along her jaw, down her neck, lingering at the collarbone. The softness of her skin under my touch was intoxicating. "You need to be properly nourished if you're to endure what I have planned for you today," I whispered, my words dripping with promise and a hint of threat.

Her breathing hitched as anticipation flickered across her face. I placed the bowl aside and focused entirely on her, my hands exploring more boldly now. Her body responded beautifully, each shiver and sigh fueling the deep satisfaction only dominance could bring me.

"Let's see just how much you can take, my pet," I murmured, increasing the intensity of the plug with a remote control. Her moans grew louder, a delightful sound that filled the room. I reveled in the power of eliciting such responses, the control I had over her pleasure.

As the vibrations intensified, so did her reactions. Her hips bucked slightly, seeking friction, seeking relief. I leaned down, my lips hovering just above hers, my breath mingling with her panting exhalations.

"Remember, you only come when I allow it," I reminded her, pulling back slightly to watch the struggle play out across her flushed face. The game of pushing her to the brink and holding her there was exhilarating, a delicious torment for both of us.

As she teetered on the edge, I pulled away completely, standing to observe the beautiful desperation I had crafted. Today was just the beginning, and I intended to explore the depths of her surrender fully. Each day would be a step deeper into our shared abyss of dark desires, and I was just as captive to this journey as she was.

With a deliberate slowness, I circled around the bed, my gaze never leaving her flushed face. The room was filled with the subtle buzz of the plug and her shallow breaths. I paused at the foot of the bed, admiring the view—her body, so open and responsive, pushed to a state of heightened sensitivity by the vibrations that coursed through her.

Reaching up, I slid my fingers along the inside of her thigh, drawing a line of fire with my touch. She tensed, her legs quivering in anticipation of where my hands might travel next. I allowed my fingertips to dance ever closer to her center, teasing the tender skin around her entrance without yet committing to touch where she most desired.

"Marianne," I called her name softly, almost a whisper, ensuring I had her full attention. She looked at me, her hazel eyes wide with need. "Focus on my voice, on my touch. Let everything else fade away."

As her gaze locked onto mine, I finally allowed my fingers to graze the edges of her entrance, not entering, just circling, playing with the edges that were slick with her arousal. The contact drew a gasp from her lips, and her body arched subtly towards my hand, silently begging for more.

I continued to trace delicate patterns, enjoying the power of holding her on this knife-edge of need. "You're doing so well, pet," I praised, my voice low and encouraging. "Just feel. Let your body respond."

Her moans became a melody that drew each of my movements in time. Each moan was a note, each gasp a chord in the symphony of our encounter.

Deciding it was time to heighten her experience, I pressed a single finger against her entrance, applying just enough pressure to promise more but not fulfilling it. Her hips bucked against the air, seeking the depth and fulfillment of a deeper touch.

"Patience, pet," I chided gently, my finger remaining firm at her entrance, poised but still. "All in good time." I wanted her desperate, teetering on the brink of madness from the pleasure, fully reliant on me to tip her over the edge.

As I maintained the teasing pressure at her entrance, my mind wandered through the complexities of our budding dynamic. I needed Marianne to be completely and irrevocably mine before I could fully reveal myself. The thought of opening up to her, of letting her see all the facets of who I am, both as her Domina and as the woman behind the facade, was fraught with vulnerability I seldom allowed myself to acknowledge.

Each careful touch, each controlled caress, was a calculated effort to bind her closer to me, not just physically but emotionally and psychologically. My fingers danced around her, promising more, always holding back enough to keep her yearning for the depth of connection that only complete surrender could offer.

"I need you to trust me, Marianne," I murmured, more to myself than to her, my voice barely audible over the hum of the vibrations and her needy desperate sounds. "Trust that I know what you need, that I can give you what you've always been searching for."

My heart throbbed with a mix of power and protective instinct as I watched her respond to my touch, her body arching and twisting with each stroke of my fingers. The control I wielded was exhilarating, intoxicating, even. The weight of it came with responsibility. I was shaping her, molding her experiences to ensure her complete devotion, her absolute belief in me as her guide and guardian.

As I continued to tease her, I was acutely aware of the delicate balance I was managing. Too much revelation too soon might scare her away, or worse, break the spell of dominance and submission that I was so carefully weaving around us. I longed for the moment when I could drop all barriers, when the trust between us would be strong enough that I could reveal my true self.

I finally let my fingers slide deep into her, eliciting a sharp intake of breath from her. The reaction she gave me was visceral, a mix of shock and pleasure that painted a portrait of raw desire on her face. As I slowly explored her, I considered the future. How would she react when she learned about me, all of me?

I will show you everything, in time, I promised silently, committing to a path that felt as dangerous as it was inevitable. My touch grew more confident, more assertive, as I resolved to forge a bond that no revelation could shatter. This was more than a game of dominance; it was a dance of souls, a negotiation of hidden truths and shared secrets. I was determined to lead us both to a place of understanding and acceptance, where the shadows of our pasts could no longer cloud the intensity of our connection.

Just as I felt her beginning to clench around my fingers, I withdrew them, letting them rest motionlessly on her clit. I lowered my mouth to her inner thigh and planted a soft kiss there. Watching her reactions intently, a smirk began to play at the corner of my mouth.

MARIANNE

Chapter 19

I wanted her fingers back inside me, craving that ecstasy again as I still teetered on the edge of pleasure. "Please, please make me cum, Domina," I pleaded, yearning to feel the coiling and tightness deep in my core and the center of my stomach.

"Greedy little pet, aren't you?" she noted with a glint in her eyes.

"Please, Domina, please," I begged, squirming and pulling at my restraints, my body aching for her touch to return. I whined in frustration and need.

Her head perked up, and her lips curled into a wide, mischievous grin. "That wasn't a pleasurable sound, pet, was it?" She stood up, standing over me, grabbing the riding crop in her hand, she started running the end of it along my neck, down my breast, across my stomach, and finally letting it hover just above my throbbing, aching, dripping wet pussy. My cunt pulsed with desire, but fear also crept through me.

I gasped as she rubbed my clit with the riding crop, and I arched into it. With a loud crack, she struck me. A hot, stinging sensation from my throbbing pussy raced through me, and my heart beat faster. I bit my tongue, holding in a squeak of surprise and pain. She tilted her head to the side. "Was that a sound of displeasure, pet?"

I shook my head violently, as I pressed my lips tightly together. When she struck my pussy again, I wiggled; the sting was sharper this time, and heat filled my core. The throbbing intensified, and I felt my clit swell.

"No more, please, Domina" I whispered sheepishly. Tears welled in the corners of my eyes, stinging them.

Domina's eyes narrowed slightly, the faintest hint of a smile playing at the corners of her mouth as she observed my reaction. "No more?" she echoed, her voice a mixture of curiosity and challenge. "But we're just beginning to explore your limits, pet."

She paused, letting the riding crop trace a slow, deliberate path down my trembling thigh, her gaze never leaving mine. The tension in the room was palpable, a heavy, charged atmosphere that seemed to buzz along my skin.

I lay there, a mix of fear and anticipation coursing through me, unsure of my own desires. As the crop's tip brushed against the inside of my knee, a shiver raced through me. She struck true on my inner thigh, eliciting a sharp inhale from the hot sting. Domina's control was absolute, her presence commanding. She knew exactly how to manipulate every response.

"Isn't this everything you wished for?" she asked me softly, her voice a seductive whisper that belied the harshness of her actions. "I am going to push you, take you to the edge. Whether you trust me or not."

Her fingers returned, sliding effortlessly over the now slick skin of my cunt, circling back to where my body ached the most. This time, her touch was gentler, almost caring, as if she were coaxing the pain to blend with pleasure. My body responded despite my conflicted mind, the earlier sting mingling with a growing heat that spread through my limbs.

"Focus on the sensations," Domina instructed, her voice low and hypnotic. "Let go of your fear. Embrace what you feel."

I breathed deeply, attempting to relax into her touch, to surrender to the complex tapestry of pain and pleasure she wove. Each thrust of her fingers into me deeper, faster, it was a careful balance, pushing me closer to a brink I both feared and longed for.

As my resistance waned and my body began to betray my trepidation, the overwhelming sensation started building into something I couldn't quite name, something powerful and all consuming. Domina watched me intently, a masterful conductor orchestrating a symphony of sensations that threatened to overwhelm me.

"Good girl," she murmured, as a moan slipped past my lips. "Let it all out, pet. Let me hear you."

Encouraged by her words, I allowed the building crescendo of pleasure to wash over me, my voice rising in tandem with the waves of intense sensations. "Fuck, Oh, God..." I gasped as tremors wracked my body and I squeezed my eyes shut, my mind awash with blinding bursts of light.

She continued her fingering of me as her thumb stroked my clit, expertly guiding me through the peaks and troughs of my arousal, demonstrating not just her dominance but her profound understanding of my hidden desires. In that moment, caught between dull pain and ecstasy, I realized I was exactly where I wanted to be.

As the waves of intense sensation gradually subsided, my breathing steadied and the room came back into focus. Her presence was a constant, comforting pressure, her mastery over this moment was evident in the gentle way she now looked down at me. The fierce storm of my emotions and aftershocks of my orgasm ebbed, leaving behind a serene calm in its wake.

She withdrew her hand slowly, and turned off the vibrations of the device she had inserted into me, then carefully removed it. The quivering relief mixed with the utter emptiness and loss of being so intensely filled was overwhelming.

The deliberate pause in sensations gave me a moment to catch my breath and steady myself. The air between us shifted as she reached for the bowl of oatmeal that had been momentarily set aside. Her movements were fluid and controlled, embodying a quiet form of dominance that was just as potent as her earlier commands.

"Now, let's finish your meal, pet," Domina said softly, her voice soothing yet laced with authority. She scooped up a spoonful of oatmeal, holding it to my lips. "Open up."

I obeyed, opening my mouth to accept the food. The warm oatmeal felt comforting, unlike the intense physical sensations I had just experienced. With each spoonful, she fed me slowly, watching me with an attentive gaze that seemed to take in every one of my subtle reactions or movements.

"Very good, just like that," she encouraged after each bite, her tone gentle, nurturing even, but firm. The simple act of being fed took on a new layer of intimacy under her control. It was clear that even this, the basic need to eat, was under her dominion.

The room was quiet except for the soft clink of the spoon against the bowl and our steady breathing. In this calm, controlled environment, I found a different kind of intensity—one that was just as compelling. The trust and surrender it required to let her feed me, to care for me in such an elemental way, deepened the bond between us, anchoring me to the present moment.

With each mouthful, I felt a deep-seated contentment. As the last of the oatmeal disappeared, Domina set the bowl aside, her eyes never leaving mine.

"There, all done," she whispered, a smile playing at the edges of her lips. "You did well, pet. Very well." Her approval washed over me, a warmth that further soothed the remnants of any turmoil within.

As she wiped a stray dab of oatmeal from my lip with a tender touch, I realized the depth of which I had been neglected and how much I craved the care. In her hands, I was being reshaped, not just enduring but thriving under her guidance and care.

DOMINA

Chapter 20

I whispered the praise against Marianne's ear, watching the flicker of warmth bloom in her eyes. "There, all done. You did well, pet. Very well." The words slipped from my lips like silk, and I meant every one of them. Seeing her soften under my touch, open and trusting, unraveled something deep inside me.

A smudge of oatmeal clung to the corner of her mouth. I wiped it away with my thumb, slower than I needed to, savoring the moment. The way she looked at me, as if the world outside these walls didn't exist. It stirred both pride and panic in equal measure. She needed this, my care, my structure and I needed it too. I needed *her* more than I cared to admit.

I ran my hands over her body again, not with hunger this time, but reverence. Every curve, every tremble, was a quiet victory. One by one, I unfastened the leather restraints. I could feel her breath hitch when the last cuff came loose. If she bolted, I would've let her, because I had to know if she *chose me.*

But she didn't run.

Instead, she wrapped herself around me like I was the only steady thing she'd ever known. I held her just as tightly, burying my face in her tangled hair, letting the scent of her skin anchor me. I curled up beside her in the bed holding on, never wanting to let her go.

For a while, we just laid there, tangled together in quiet surrender. I hummed a lullaby my mother used to sing when I was small. I had no idea if Marianne recognized the tune, but it calmed something in both of us.

Eventually, I kissed her forehead and pulled back, brushing a loose strand of hair behind her ear. "Pet, you need to rest," I said, my voice low but firm. "I'm going to leave you to do that now. Be a good girl for me."

Even as I rose, I felt her body resist the absence. And, mine did too.

The moment I closed the door behind me, the quiet snick of the lock echoing too loudly in my ears, I knew she was all I would ever want. The key, warm from resting against my chest all day, slid smoothly into place as I secured it once more around my neck. It lay heavy between my breasts, a reminder of her, of the girl tucked beneath my roof, soft, bruised, and willingly tethered to me.

I allowed myself one long exhale before heading up to my bedroom.

Tonight was demo night.

It wasn't something I wanted to attend, not really. Well, at least not by myself anyway. I needed the familiarity, the ritual. The dungeon was a space where the world made sense. Where the dance of power had rules and expectations and a safe place I could be who I truly was in public.

Flicking on the vanity light, I opened the wardrobe doors and ran my fingers across the cool metal zippers, the rich leather, and the sharp lines of tailored lace. I selected a black underbust corset with red piping, stiff-boned and worn in all the right places. The satin hugged my waist and pushed up the soft curve of my breasts, which I paired with a mesh bodysuit that left little to the imagination and thigh-high patent boots that clicked with every step. I ran my finger along a collar, it was a deep oxblood leather with brass fastenings, before grabbing my ruby rhinestone choker. I clasped the necklace on and added a pair of fingerless gloves.

118

As I turned to the full-length mirror, I didn't see Jenny, the woman burdened with deadlines and demanding clients. I saw Domina, composed, cruel, calculated, and merciful.

Good. I needed that tonight.

I moved to the small case on my dresser and opened it with reverence. Nestled inside were my tools. My instruments. My art.

The violet wand rested in the center, its coiled glass attachments glinting under the soft light. I ran a cloth over each piece as I prepped the attachments—the comb, the mushroom, and the little bulb I reserved for the most delicate work. I packed it carefully, adding my conductive paddle and a grounding pad, and zipped the case shut with the care of a surgeon sealing a patient.

There was power in electricity.

Unseen but felt. Feared. Craved.

I slipped my arm into a leather coat, the one with a deep split in the back and just enough menace in the shoulders, and gave myself one last look in the mirror. Everything about me screamed control, except the flicker of doubt I caught in my own eyes.

I swallowed it down.

Tonight, I would spark lightning into willing skin. I would make strangers moan with nothing more than a whisper of current. Just maybe, it would quiet the part of me that couldn't stop thinking about the girl downstairs.

The girl who had asked to be saved.

The girl who, for the first time in a long time, I wanted to keep but didn't fully trust that I could.

I headed to the rented bar space we used for our events. It wasn't a long drive, and I was grateful not to be left alone with my own thoughts for too long.

The low hum of music and hushed murmurs wrapped around me the moment I stepped into the dungeon. Fluorescent lights buzzed faintly above, softened by red gels that bathed the space in a warm, deviant glow. The scent of leather, sweat, and anticipation clung to every breath. About a hundred bodies mingled in the open industrial bar space, some in latex, others in corsets and chains, and a few newcomers in little more than nerves and curiosity.

Multiple demo stations had been set up along the perimeter. Rope suspension near the far wall, a spanking bench beside the mirrored column, and across the room, a shibari performance that had already drawn a small, reverent crowd. I offered nods of recognition to a few familiar faces, Doms and subs I'd worked with, taught, or once collared, briefly, before they too had slipped away.

None of them mattered tonight.

Only *she* did.

I couldn't stop thinking about Marianne.

I imagined her here—eyes wide, chest rising in shallow breaths as she took it all in for the first time. I'd guide her hand to the violet wand. Let her feel the vibration in her palm, the crackle in the air. I'd show her how it made even the most stoic of men arch and moan like they'd been touched by fire and ghost kisses.

She would look so fucking radiant bound to the wooden cross in a demo, trembling from both pleasure and stage fright, blushing when I whispered filth in her ear for the crowd to hear. Every inch of her would be on display, every reaction mine to pull from her. The sound the bullwhip would make marking her flesh. My eyes fluttered closed as I heard the crack sound loudly over the crowd.

One day, I thought. *One day, she'll kneel at my feet in front of all of them, and they'll see who she belongs to.*

"Domina."

I blinked, brought back to the moment by a familiar submissive. Jonny had been a platonic play partner for years. He approached, already stripped to the waist and wearing a leather posture collar. I hoped he would one day find the Dom man of his dreams.

"Still leading the violet wand demo tonight?" he asked, hopeful.

"Yes," I replied, my voice cool and firm. "Station three."

The crowd had already gathered near my table as I approached, the metal case in hand. I set it down and opened it like a priest unveiling sacred tools. The violet wand drew its usual fascinated whispers, and I explained the currents, the electrodes, the science masked by seduction.

But even as I moved through the motions—Demonstrating, explaining, watching Jonny gasp when I grazed his thigh with a low-voltage flicker—*I wasn't there.*

I was downstairs, in my home, where Marianne lay cocooned in blankets I had chosen for her. My sweet pet, fragile and mine.

The room applauded when Jonny dropped to his knees, his body still shivering from the last pass of static energy along his spine. I smiled, nodded, and gave my final safety pointers.

However, my mind remained haunted by the phantom of Marianne's soft sighs.

By the fantasy of her begging for more.

By the vision of the girl I would one day bring here, not just to train, not just to show off…

Because she was *mine*.

MARIANNE

Chapter 21

After Domina finished cleaning me, her soft hands caressed my body with a tenderness that caught me off guard. She reached for the restraints, releasing my right wrist first, followed by the left, and then my feet. I could have run; perhaps I should have run. Instead, I wrapped my arms around her neck, drawing her close and breathing in her scent. Tears pricked my eyes as I clung to her, her arms wrapping securely around my waist. She held me gently and in that embrace, I realized how touch-starved I had been. I never wanted to leave. I wanted to stay in her arms forever.

She softly laid me back down and settled onto the mattress next to me, her soft humming the only sound in the quiet space. I don't know how long we lay there tangled together, but it wasn't long enough. She kissed my forehead and spoke softly, yet with a firm tone. "Pet, you need to rest. I am going to leave you to do that now. Be a good girl and rest for me."

Panic filled me, not because I felt trapped but because she was leaving me alone, and I didn't want to be alone. That fear always gripped me; I had always felt alone but never knew how to be truly, safely alone with my own thoughts. I was always expected to care for someone, to do something. Here, my only purpose was to rest, and I didn't know how to just do that.

She stood and tucked me under the quilt again, leaving me alone in the room with only my thoughts, my feelings, and myself. I heard the click of the lock as she exited, and shadows washed over the room, with only the dim light of a lamp filling the space. With no sense of time and no immediate needs, I was uncertain whether to sleep, search for a way to escape, or simply explore the space. My thoughts flooded in, overwhelming me.

As silence settled heavily around me, the faint hum of the lamp became a companion in the quiet. I lay still, the quilt's weight comforting yet constrictive, mirroring the turmoil inside me. Curiosity nudged at my anxiety. What lay beyond this room, within these walls that held both safety and captivity?

With a hesitant breath, I decided to rise. Sliding carefully out from under the quilt, I let my feet touch the cool floor. I grabbed up the quilt and wrapped it around my naked body. Not having clothes was unsettling but also freeing. The room felt larger and more imposing by night, shadows stretching across the sparse furnishings like dark fingers reaching out.

I moved slowly, my steps tentative as I approached the nearest wall. Running my hands along it, I searched for any irregularity, any signs of weakness that might offer an opportunity for escape. Yet, there was a part of me, a quiet voice, wondering if I truly wanted to find one.

The room offered small clues about its purpose and its previous occupants: a faded mark where a picture might have hung, a slight discoloration on the floor where furniture had been moved. Each detail felt like a whisper of stories untold.

There was a small bathroom in the far corner I hadn't noticed until now. It had no door but just a simple toilet, sink, and shower. I walked in and used it before continuing to explore the soft lit space.

Finally, I approached the door. Locked and solid, it stood as a firm reminder of my reality. The cold metal of the handle sent a shiver through me—not just from the chill but from the realization of my isolation.

I turned away from the door, my heart heavy. Perhaps, tomorrow I would find the courage or the means to leave, but tonight, I was not ready. The room, with its low light and stretching shadows, felt less like a prison and more like a sanctuary from a world I wasn't sure I was prepared to face.

Returning to bed, I crawled back under the quilt. The fabric embraced me softly, a silent reassurance. As I lay there, the overwhelming thoughts began to ebb, replaced by a weary acceptance. Sleep, elusive before, now beckoned with a gentle hand. In the quiet of the room, with the soft hum of the lamp as my lullaby, I finally let my eyes close as my mind drifted to what happened last week.

"Did you mop this floor on your hands and knees?" My mother's accusing tone sliced through me like a blade, and I nodded in silence. I stood there in the shapeless, itchy clothes she'd picked up for me at a thrift store the day before, baggy, rough, and thoroughly unflattering. According to her, they were the only "respectable" things she could find in my size.

New clothes had always been a rare luxury, and even then, they came after grueling hours of trying on outfit after outfit, most too tight or too matronly. If something didn't cover every inch of me to her satisfaction, it was dismissed immediately. Anything that hinted at my cleavage was forbidden. Dresses and skirts were mandatory, no pants, and the hem had to fall below my knees but not quite to my ankles. As for my shoulders, even a whisper of bare skin was too much; every top had to have sleeves at least two inches wide. Finding clothes that met her impossible standards and actually fit my body? Nearly impossible.

I shifted on my feet in front of her as she scrutinized the kitchen floor. Apparently, we were having company for dinner—a young man whom our pastor had mentioned was interested in finding a wife soon. My mother had managed to insert herself into their conversation to invite him over to meet me, their perfectly chaste daughter. His glance and the unsettling, wicked smile he gave me when he accepted the invitation had left me feeling uneasy.

"Now do it again. It isn't gleaming. We should be able to eat off it because it's so clean," she commanded. My stomach grumbled at the mention of food, drawing a sharp look from my mother.

I averted my eyes, focusing on the floor as I slowly dropped to my knees. My mother tossed a wet rag in front of me, and I began wiping the floors again, scrubbing the already clean surface as tears welled up in my eyes, burning at the corners.

The scent of the cleaning solution mingled with the dust motes dancing in the sunlight that filtered through the kitchen window, an oppressive reminder of my constrained existence. Each pass of the rag across the linoleum felt like an erasure of myself, scrubbing away parts of my identity with every swipe.

As I moved methodically across the floor, a childhood memory flashed through my mind—a time when the kitchen had been a place of laughter and warmth, not just of expectations and reprimands. I remembered being small enough to sit on the counter, swinging my legs, watching my mother bake cookies. Back then, she sang along to the radio, her voice light and carefree. How had we drifted so far from those days?

The sound of the back door opening jolted me from my reverie. I stiffened, scrubbing harder, anticipating my mother's sharp voice or the guest's arrival. Though, it was neither. Instead, my father walked in, his work boots leaving fresh tracks on the wet floor I had just cleaned. He paused, noticing the tension in my posture.

"What's all this?" he asked, his tone weary as he surveyed the scene—me on the floor, the rag in my hand, and my red, swollen eyes.

Before I could respond, my mother interjected from the doorway, "Just making sure she learns the importance of a clean home, especially with the guest we're having tonight. It's important that she makes a good impression."

My father nodded, seemingly approving her words. He then sighed, wiping the sweat from his brow. "It's been a long day at work, and I'm hoping dinner will be ready soon. I could use a good meal." His voice carried a hint of impatience, underscoring his focus on his own needs rather than the scene before him.

He didn't offer to help me up. Instead, he walked past me to the refrigerator, leaving me to finish my task alone. The brief hope that he might understand or intervene evaporated as quickly as it had appeared.

The gap between the memories of simpler yet suffocating times and my current reality widened, leaving me feeling more conflicted than ever. I finally let the peace of the night take me into a deep sleep.

DOMINA

Chapter 22

The fluorescent lights of the diner buzzed overhead, a steady white hum that matched the clink of forks against ceramic and the occasional raucous laughter from a booth near the bathrooms where a group of college kids were clearly riding the tail end of a night out.

Jonny was already at our usual booth, tucked in the back corner beneath a buzzing wall sconce. He looked like a piece of pastel art dropped into a black-and-white photograph—lanky frame, pale blue sweater, baby blue eyes still rimmed with eyeliner, and that perfectly styled crop of black hair that defied gravity and humidity.

I slid into the red vinyl booth across from him, and he was already halfway through a strawberry milkshake. The table was sticky despite the napkin dispenser's best efforts to look sterile. He gave me a grin over the rim of his glass, pink whipped cream smudging the corner of his mouth.

"You're late, Mistress of the Dark Arts," he teased, his eyes glinting. "I thought you were going to ghost me like one of your 'I crave structure' subs."

"Funny," I said dryly, waving off a waitress who gave me the once-over before returning to her pot of stale coffee. "I got cornered by that rope-top from last month's workshop. Again."

"God, the clingy one," he said with a dramatic shudder. "Like, sir, I agreed to one scene and a respectful goodbye—not a post-scene memoir."

I chuckled and leaned back, letting the tension bleed out of my shoulders. "You're glowing, by the way. That impact demo we did made you the star tonight."

"Oh please," he waved a hand.. "You're the reason half the room stayed past eleven. Watching you hold a wand like it's part of your soul? *Erotic*. Half the femmes looked ready to renounce monogamy and throw themselves at your boots."

I snorted, not bothering to deny it. "Still, it's always better when you're my demo bunny. You don't flinch like the newbies."

Jonny grinned around his straw, clearly pleased with himself. He had been my demo bunny for both of my intro scenes tonight—first for the violet wand station and later for the spanking bench rotation. Trustworthy, responsive, and unflappable, he was the perfect partner to showcase technique without drama.

Tonight had been an open house night at the club, which meant new faces, fresh curiosity, and plenty of nerves. After the official demos were finished with trusted members like Jonny, we opened the floor to volunteers—eager hopefuls who wanted to try out the sensations and maybe, just maybe, find their place in our world.

"Because I trust you, duh." He sipped his shake and tilted his head. "We've been doing this—what, four years?"

"Almost five," I said.

He nodded. "You're still the only person I'll bottom for in public. You get the vibe just right, firm but never cruel. And, you know not to sexualize me."

"I'd sooner fuck a turnip," I deadpanned.

"That's what makes it perfect!" he grinned, pointing a long finger at me. "You're a hard-ass with boundaries. It's why we work. I get the catharsis, you get to look hot and powerful, and no one ends up crying afterward—unless it's part of the scene."

Our waitress finally arrived, a tired-looking woman with smeared eyeliner and a notepad. I ordered a chamomile tea and a slice of apple pie. Jonny added an order of seasoned fries "for balance."

As she shuffled away, Jonny leaned on one elbow, twisting his spoon between his fingers. "I've been thinking about what my ideal Master would be like."

"Oh?" I arched my brow.

"Yeah. Like… I think I want someone older. Not necessarily a Daddy…God, no, but someone solid. Someone who knows who they are, owns a proper toolset, can hold eye contact without trying to flirt, you know?"

I hummed. "A real grown-up."

"Exactly," he said, nodding. "And I don't need them to be rich or have a dungeon—though a nice loft with wall hooks wouldn't hurt. I just want to be seen, Jenny. I want to be worshipped in the right way. Held down and lifted up at the same time."

His words struck something in me. I thought of Marianne's eyes when she looked at me like I could rewrite her entire existence. Like I had already started to. The way she trembled, not in fear but in conflict—between what she'd been told to want and what her body begged for.

Jonny nodded slowly. "I think I just want someone who'll give me that look—you know the one. Like you're their whole goddamn world. Like they'll follow you into the fire just because you told them to."

I tilted my head, watching him. "Have you ever had that?"

He shook his head, a wistful smile ghosting his lips. "Almost. But I think I loved the fantasy of it more than the person."

"She looks at me like that," I said, almost to myself.

Jonny tilted his head. "Who?"

I hesitated, then gave him a soft smile. "A girl. New. She's… she's not like the others."

My chest tightened, thinking of Marianne—her eyes, wide and hopeful, the raw need in her voice when she said please. She didn't even know how perfectly she fit. How right she felt in my hands. It was terrifying. Beautiful. Addictive.

"But she doesn't know yet," I said quietly.

Jonny's brows lifted. "Oh?"

I hesitated. "She will. It's just she doesn't understand what she is yet. What she needs. She's still tangled up in everything the world told her she had to be."

His gaze softened, more curious than judgmental. "And, you're going to help her figure it out?"

I smiled. "I already am."

Jonny's eyes filled with concern but he didn't press. "Just don't break her. Or, let her break you."

Our food arrived, greasy and comforting. I picked at the pie, my mind already turning back toward home, to the girl wrapped in blankets in my bed, who didn't even know what kind of leash she was already on.

Jonny nudged my foot under the table. "So... when do I get to meet her?"

I smirked. "When she's ready. When *I'm* sure she won't run."

He nodded, respectful. "You'll know. You always do."

As the diner's jukebox crackled to life again, I let myself believe—if only for a moment—that he was right.

We fell into silence for a few moments, eating, the warmth of the pie and tea dulling the sharp edges inside me. Still, my thoughts pulled like a tether back home—back to her.

I would return soon, back to the girl who owned more of me then I even knew. Back to the choice I had made. Back to the risk.

For now, I let the sweetness linger. Jonny, bless him, didn't push. He knew the game. He knew the lines we crossed—some in neon, some in shadow. And he knew that, in the end, what we all really wanted... was to belong to someone completely.

MARIANNE

Chapter 23

A bell rang, stirring me into consciousness and pulling me abruptly from my dreams. "Good morning, pet." Her sweet voice coaxed a smile onto my face before I could resist it.

"Morning," I managed to say softly, my throat dry and aching from the depth of my sleep. My eyes briefly landed on a tray set on a small table, laden with water, pancakes, and eggs, but quickly returned to Domina. She stood in an electric blue corset and a mini skirt, her thigh-high boots accentuating her height and commanding presence. Her arms were crossed, and in one hand, she held a thick red stick. In that moment, I was utterly struck by her presence.

"Today, we shall teach you all about your new expectations." She gave me a smirk that sent a shiver down my spine, mingling fear with excitement. Clutching the quilt around my naked body, I sat up fully in the bed.

She stepped closer, leaning in close to my ear, she purred. "You are going to learn how to be my very good girl."

She brought the red wand close to my ear and pressed the button. I heard the unmistakable snap of electricity, the sharp scent of ozone curling into my nostrils. "If you don't do as you're told, or if you do it wrong, you'll be *reminded*," she whispered, her tone shifting to something stern and commanding. Her breath was hot against my neck, sending a shiver straight down my spine.

Domina stood back, her back straight, and in a commanding, husky voice that made my core coil and wetness gather between my thighs, she said, "Stand and present yourself to me. When I say 'present', you face me and stand with your feet shoulder-width apart, your hands straight out, palms up."

My legs trembled, uncertain and weak beneath me, but I obeyed. I stood and turned to face her, my body fully exposed. Heat bloomed in my cheeks as a line of arousal trickled slowly down the inside of my thighs.

Her gaze raked over me, piercing, deliberate. However, there was something softer hidden in her eyes… a flicker of approval that made my breath catch. She circled me slowly, the clack of her booted heels echoing through the room, every step heightening the tension coiling in my belly.

"You're doing well, pet," she said at last. Her voice carried both reassurance and authority, wrapping around me like silk and steel. The praise soothed the edge of my nerves, but the excitement buzzing beneath my skin only grew stronger.

She stopped in front of me again. "Next is forward present," she instructed. "It's similar, but this time, you'll cup your hands beneath your breasts and lift them. Nipples forward."

I swallowed hard, anxiety tightening my throat. I reached up and cupped each heavy breast, struggling to keep them lifted and aligned. My nipples, already stiff, didn't quite point forward the way I wanted. I fumbled with my grip, frustrated and flustered.

Domina closed the distance between us. The zap of the wand buzzed next to my cheek with a sharp, electric snap that made me jolt and gasp.

"Here, pet. Like this." Her hands settled over mine, guiding them to the outer curves of my breasts. She splayed my fingers wide, her thumbs brushing teasingly over my nipples, making me shudder. "There. Now… don't move."

She stepped back again, beginning another slow, measured circle. Her boots clicked against the floor with a rhythm that matched the pounding in my chest. I stood frozen, burning with embarrassment and need. The cool air licked at my skin, each second stretching longer than the last.

The tip of the red wand traced down my collarbone, then slipped between the valley of my breasts, gliding lower across my stomach and down between my legs, where her touch dipped into my wetness. I whimpered, trembling, and she dragged it down the inside of my thigh. Every nerve in my body lit up in response, and I gasped—utterly helpless and undeniably hers.

"Pet, do you know what this is in my hand?" she cooed, her voice low and teasing, laced with seductive promise. I shook my head, not daring to move or speak, my breath catching as she lifted the red stick to my breast and lightly traced it over my nipple, teasing it.

"This is called an electro zapper," she said, her voice silky with wicked delight. "It has three settings, and this button delivers a shock. Painful, but not harmful—think of it like a cattle prod for humans. When used in the right places, especially the sensitive ones, it gives just enough of a jolt to push you right over the edge."

She smiled, clearly proud of that fact. I swallowed hard, doing my best not to move, but my hands trembled, and my breast slipped out of position.

Click.

I cried out. The sharp sting was more startling than painful, but the sudden loss of breath from my lungs left me gasping. I quickly tried to correct my mistake and reposition myself, but the glint in her eye and the smirk curling on her lips told me she liked how I'd reacted. Swallowing my nerves, I settled back into position.

"Good. Now, 'down present' is the last position for today," she instructed. "You'll kneel, sit back on your heels, place your palms face-up on your thighs, and keep your eyes on me."

It was a lot to remember, but I obeyed, dropping to my knees without hesitation. Oh, how I loved looking up at her from this position, every inch of her radiating control, power, and something that made my pulse quicken.

Domina stepped closer, her boots clicking softly on the floor as she circled me again. I sat exactly as instructed, knees pressed together, back straight, palms resting gently on my thighs, eyes lifted to meet hers. My whole body hummed with the effort to remain perfectly still.

She towered above me like a storm about to break, her presence magnetic, every inch of her draped in authority. Beneath that strength, I saw something else in her eyes, something deeper. Satisfaction. Possession. Pride.

"You look exquisite like this, pet," she murmured, reaching out to trace her fingers down my cheek, across my jaw, and finally tilting my chin just a little higher. "So eager to please... and learning so fast. I wonder—" she leaned down slightly, her lips just above my ear, her breath warm against my skin, "—how long you've been waiting for someone to tell you exactly what to do."

I swallowed hard, my lips parting but no words forming. I didn't have an answer, not one that wouldn't shatter whatever pride I had left.

She didn't seem to need one.

Domina straightened, stepping back and folding her arms as she looked me over once more, her gaze slow and deliberate.

"I could spend hours molding you," she said, almost to herself, her voice edged with something darker, almost reverent. "And, I will. Piece by piece. Touch by touch."

She dragged a chair behind me with a slow, deliberate scrape of wood against the floor. Her voice dropped, thick with sultry command. "Now you'll earn your breakfast."

She placed one booted foot on the seat, lifting her leg and revealing herself —bare, glistening, and utterly divine. No panties beneath the short skirt she wore. My breath caught as her heat radiated only inches from my face, and I shuddered at the raw, unapologetic beauty of her pussy.

Her hand found the back of my head, fingers threading gently through my tangled hair. The contrast between her tenderness and her dominance made my stomach twist with an aching need.

"Show me you can make me come, pet." Her words echoed through my mind, sending a wave of nerves fluttering in my stomach like a swarm of butterflies. She guided my head closer to her center, and I breathed in her scent, rich, heady, intoxicating.

My lips parted, and I tasted her slowly, reverently, letting the flavor of her spread across my tongue. I squeezed my eyes shut, overwhelmed by the raw intimacy of it. God help me, I loved this. Being on my knees for her, worshiping her with my mouth, the weight of her hand tangled in my hair grounding me in this moment.

I started to lift my hand from my thigh, greedy for more of her—

Click.

I jolted as the sharp zap struck my arm.

"No," she said firmly. "To move from this position without permission earns correction. Worship me with your mouth, and only your mouth."

"Yes, Domina." The words left me quickly, instinctively. That was one of the first things she had taught me during our late-night chats, *always* address her properly.

I refocused, dragging my tongue over her clit, then slowly tracing the edges of her lips before delving into her depths. I moaned softly into her, the taste of her only fueling my own hunger. Each breath I took was laced with her scent, my own arousal building with every stroke of my tongue. Her soft groans and gasps above me spurred me on.

"Ooh, fuck...right there, pet. That's my good girl," she moaned, her voice thick with pleasure. "Suck me in, between your teeth—ohh..."

Her fingers fisted in my hair, anchoring me in place as her hips bucked forward, meeting the rhythm of my mouth with wild need. I lost myself in her completely.

DOMINA

Chapter 24

I never did this. *Ever.*

My pleasure was almost always drawn from theirs, the rush of power, the absolute control I wielded over my submissives. Their obedience, their trembling anticipation, their surrender to my will... that was what drove me. Watching someone unravel under my command or teeter on the edge because I kept them there—that was satisfaction. That was enough.

Letting someone touch me like this, bring me to my own undoing? That was something else entirely. Something far more dangerous.

Maybe it wasn't just about control. Maybe it was that as much as they trusted me with their bodies, I never truly trusted them with mine, with my needs, or my vulnerabilities. That level of openness felt like exposure, like weakness. I didn't allow weakness.

This...this was different.

My breath caught in my throat. The sensation was primal, raw. A new kind of hunger clawed its way through me, one I didn't know had been hiding all this time.

I stood over her, my left foot anchored on the chair behind her, steadying myself. Marianne knelt below me, lips parted, eyes reverent. I held her face close, guiding her mouth to where I throbbed with need, wet, aching, open.

When her teeth grazed my clit, I groaned. Loud, real, and unfiltered. A shudder tore through me.

Part of me wanted to stop her. I wanted to hold on to the last thread of control over myself.

I didn't stop her. I let her keep going. I drew her closer.

I felt the peak of my climax approaching, the tension winding tight in my core. My stomach clenched, and I fisted her hair, pulling her closer—so close I barely cared if she could breathe. In that moment, all that mattered was claiming her, marking her in this way.

I had never done this before. Not like this.

Because she wasn't just mine.

Fuck— I was hers, too.

My whole body quaked as I came, the orgasm crashing over me harder than I'd expected. I held her there against me, savoring the way she began to struggle, tugging at my grip, silently begging for air. After a few breathless moments, I finally pulled her head back, arching her neck as she gasped, her face glistening with my release.

Fuck, I wanted to throw her down on this hard floor and fuck her until she begged me to stop. Until she was sure she couldn't cum again. Until I nearly broke her.

Instead, I simply held her there, gazing into her wide eyes with my feral smile stretching across my lips.

"Such a good girl for me, my pet," I cooed.

I leaned down and licked her face, the tip of her nose, the curve of her jaw, before pulling her up to stand in front of me. Then, I kissed her.

I never kissed my submissives, but I loved kissing her. I couldn't help myself, couldn't resist tasting her sweetness, feeling her tongue twist and tangle with mine, breathing her in like she was the air I'd been starving for. Her moans and whimpers vibrated into my mouth, only fueling the wildfire of my need.

When I finally pulled away, I was breathless. She stood there, flushed and needy, her lips swollen and kiss-drunk.

"Eat your breakfast. You earned it. Then shower," I said, my voice tight, controlled, as I pulled a stool out from under the small table. I couldn't let her see just how deeply she affected me, how utterly owned I already was. I'd give her anything she asked for. Anything.

I watched her as she lowered herself back down onto the stool I had placed for her, hands trembling slightly as she reached for the spoon. The steam from pancakes, and eggs curled upward, catching the soft light, and her eyes flicked up to mine as she took the first bite. Obedient. Beautiful. Mine.

She ate in silence, each motion delicate and deliberate, as if she were afraid to break whatever spell had been cast between us. Her lashes were still damp from the tears I hadn't kissed away, and her cheeks were flushed, whether from pleasure or shame, I wasn't entirely sure. Maybe both. Maybe that was what made her perfect.

I circled behind her, watching her from every angle, my gaze tracing the lines of her back, the soft curve of her shoulder. Her body bore the memory of me, marks I had left, imprints of my control, echoes of my care. Her presence soothed something in me, something I hadn't even realized that I had been aching for.

But beneath the calm, beneath the warm afterglow of power exchanged, a flicker of unease stirred in my gut. This was too close. Too much.

I'd never allowed anyone this far in. Not emotionally. Not physically. Not like this.

I had seen so many walk away, willing at first, then frightened of what they wanted, of who they became when they surrendered. They would call me dangerous. They would say I twisted them. The truth was, I only ever showed them the pieces they kept buried, the shadows they feared.

Now… she was cracking something inside me open.

I clenched my hands behind my back and straightened my spine, pushing the vulnerability down where it belonged. Locked beneath the surface, where it couldn't touch me.

She was almost finished eating.

I moved to the cabinet and retrieved a neatly folded robe from the top shelf. Soft, deep burgundy, warm. I draped it over my arm and returned to her side.

"Stand," I said, voice smooth but laced with iron. "I'll show you to the shower."

She looked up at me with those wide, searching eyes. Still questioning. Still so full of trust it made my chest ache.

When she rose to her feet, I slipped the robe over her shoulders and gently tugged it closed around her body. My fingers lingered on the knot of the belt.

She stood still, waiting for permission. For praise. For whatever I would give her next.

I leaned in, my mouth grazing her ear. "You were exceptional, pet," I whispered. "You're everything I hoped you'd be."

And that terrified me.

MARIANNE

Chapter 25

My heart was racing. I didn't want food, or care, or comfort. I wanted her, all of her. I wanted to feel her inside me again, to soothe the ache that still throbbed deep in my core. She tasted so sweet, so perfect, and watching her come undone on my tongue only intensified my need.

My pussy still pulsed, empty and desperate, each beat echoing with craving. My thighs were slick, sticky with evidence of my desire, and shame clung to me like a second skin.

Fucksake, I was going to hell. I knew it, I was sinful. And I didn't care anymore.

Well… mostly.

The robe she'd wrapped me in was soft, warm, and clung to my skin in all the places that reminded me what had just happened. Domina said nothing as she guided me to the shower. A small, open space tucked into the corner of the room with no door, no curtain, no privacy. Just smooth tile and the heavy weight of being seen.

She turned on the water, and steam rose instantly.

I loosened the robe in front of her, letting it slip open, and then reached for her hand. Without hesitation, I guided it between my thighs, pressing her fingers against the heat and wetness there.

A flicker of surprise crossed her face, quick and fleeting, before a smirk of dark amusement curled at the corner of her lips.

"Is my pet a needy, greedy little thing?" she murmured, her voice low and taunting.

I bit my lower lip, nodding as heat surged through me. "Please," I breathed, my voice barely more than a whisper.

"Get into the shower, pet." Her hand left the heat of my aching cunt and moved to test the water, letting the spray cascade over her fingers.

Everything in me didn't want a shower. I wanted release. I wanted her touch, I needed it. My body pulsed with frustration, and I crossed my arms defiantly.

"No, Domina," I said, louder than I meant to, my voice trembling. "I didn't actually agree to this." I gestured wildly around the room, panic starting to rise.

She turned slightly, casting me a look from the corner of her eye, her face unreadable. My chest tightened. Fear prickled down my spine, but I pushed forward anyway.

"We talked… about a lot of things, but I never agreed to… this." I motioned to the restraints, the space, the dynamic now made real. "I mean… you are my Domina, the one I've been talking to online for months, right?"

The words hung heavy in the air, like I'd just popped a fragile bubble neither of us wanted to acknowledge. The fantasy had fractured, reality rushing in to fill the space between us.

She turned to face me fully then, one hand sliding to her hip, the other trailing along the curve of her blue satin corset. Her gaze was steady, unreadable. She said nothing.

She took a step closer, and I instinctively stepped back. Her smirk deepened. She kept advancing, slow and deliberate, until my back hit the cool tile beside the rushing stream of the shower. I froze.

152

Her hand rose to my neck, fingers spreading wide, her thumb brushing softly along my jaw. The contrast of her gentle touch and firm grip sent a tremor through me.

Leaning in, her voice dropped to a low, dangerous murmur. "And, if I wasn't... what then, pet?"

Fear and arousal twisted together inside me, my breath catching in my throat. My heart pounded as my body betrayed me, trembling not just with uncertainty, but with desire.

"Didn't you need someone to save you?" Her voice was low, almost tender, but her grip around my throat remained firm. I tried to swallow, feeling the pressure of her hand against the movement, and gave a small nod. Because I did.

I couldn't save myself. I hadn't been strong enough. I wasn't sure I ever would be.

"Do you want to leave?" she whispered, her tone laced with a cruel kind of mercy—as if freedom were hers to grant.

My eyes fluttered shut, tears stinging at the corners. Did I want to leave?

No. Not when I wanted more. Not when I wanted her. When I wanted all of this, every dark, and twisted thing.

"No." The word escaped me, firm and raw, the truth in it undeniable.

Her gaze didn't waver. "Then you consent to this? To me? To all of it?" Her voice was steady, serious, and commanding.

She was giving me an out.

This was my moment to choose. If I said yes, there'd be no more hiding behind the veil of being taken, no safety in the lie of being a victim. Saying yes meant ownership, of the desire, the surrender, the dark craving that lived inside me.

If I said yes… I would no longer be innocent.

Not ever again.

"Yes, Domina." I opened my eyes as the words left my lips, a single tear slipping down my cheek. I held her gaze, unflinching, open, and fully surrendered.

She kissed me, hard and firm, but not deep. It was a seal, not a promise.

Then, her hand fisted in my hair, and she yanked me from the wall and away from the shower in one swift, unrelenting motion.

"Ah—fuck, what the hell…" The protest tore from me more in shock than defiance.

I stumbled, feet slipping against the damp tile, and barely caught my balance before she dragged me toward the bed. In the next breath, I was hauled over her knees, bent forward, hair still in her grip. My feet no longer touched the floor, and I flung my arms out, palms smacking the cold concrete to keep from slamming into it face-first.

I panted, breath ragged, my pulse roaring in my ears. My heart hammered against my ribs like a drumbeat of anticipation and fear — and want.

I felt her other hand glide up the back of my thigh, over the curve of my ass, and then lift the robe, baring me completely. A moment later, the sharp sting of her palm cracked across my cheek, hard and deliberate.

I yelped, the sound escaping before I could stop it. The ache deep in my core only intensified, a throbbing need swelling inside me. I clenched, trying to suppress the rising tide building with every touch, every strike.

I knew I had stepped out of line, that I had pushed back. Not that I regretted it, and certainly not that I hadn't expected consequences. But what I hadn't expected was how much I would *want* them... how much I would *need* them.

DOMINA

Chapter 26

She knew, and she chose me. Relief flooded my chest, warm and all-consuming, quickly followed by a surge of pride. That didn't mean she'd get away with running, with backing away from me, from telling me no.

She had submitted. Now, she would learn exactly what that meant.

I had been patient, caring, even. I teased, coaxed, guided her into my world gently. But fuck, I *loved* punishment. I *thrived* in it. The adrenaline, the fear, the delicious crackle of obedience earned through pain—it fed something darker inside me. Something I kept hidden from the world, masked behind seductive smiles and calculated restraint.

But not from her. Not anymore.

Now, I would show her just a glimpse of that shadow, a taste of the fire that burned under my control. And, when I was done, she would know exactly what to expect when she disobeyed.

I brought my hand down hard and firm, each smack landing with precision across her full, vulnerable ass. Delicious red marks bloomed beneath my palm, proof of my control. I spread my fingers wide, striking for maximum impact, alternating sides with practiced rhythm. She jerked with each slap, her cries sharp, pained yips and helpless yowls that only fed my hunger.

I was going to bring her to tears. Break her down, strip her bare. And when I was done, I'd drag her into the cold spray of the shower and fuck her until she knew—*truly* knew—she was mine.

My grip tangled tighter in her messy, sweat-damp hair, keeping her in place as she squirmed beneath me, her body trembling with the effort of endurance. My desire surged hotter, molten now, every strike of my hand igniting that wildfire inside me.

"You're going to take your spanking properly. Stop moving, pet." I paused, rubbing the red-hot marks I left across her plump, perfect butt. My nails grazed her heated flesh, and she moaned.

She actually *moaned.*

A wicked grin curled at my lips as I slipped my fingers between her cheeks. She was so wet, slick with desire. The proof of her arousal made me chuckle low in my throat before I clicked my tongue in mock disappointment.

"You'll give me your tears before you scream my name, pet." My voice etched with my own desire.

I raised my soaked hand and brought it down again—*smack*—the sound cracked through the room. Her body jolted.

"Ten more," I said, my voice velvet-wrapped steel. "But you'll take them willingly. Over the bed. With the belt. Do you understand?"

She shuddered in my grip, goosebumps rising on her skin as I straightened her up. Her breath escaped in a stuttering exhale.

"Yes, Domina," she whimpered.

I stripped the robe from her body—what little still clung to it—and pointed to the bed. With trembling steps, she moved, bent over the edge, presenting her ass to me, perfect and obedient.

"Good girl," I murmured, praise rolling off my tongue like silk.

I let her lie there exposed, and waiting, while I retrieved the leather belt from a locked cupboard across the room. My booted heels clicked against the floor, the sharp rhythm, the sound mixing with the still running water, and her rapid, shallow breaths.

I folded the belt in half and snapped it against itself with a loud *crack.*

She jumped, trembling, and I couldn't help but smile.

I approached slowly, letting the anticipation build, and ran my hand gently down the curve of her back, steadying her. "Ten strokes. Count them down for me, pet," I instructed, my voice low and commanding.

I let the heavy leather dangle from my hand, the weight familiar and comforting. Pulling back, I raised my arm, ready to strike. The anticipation of the marks I would leave, the cries she would make, coiled something tight and dark deep inside me.

I let the tension go in a swift, precise motion as the belt struck across both cheeks. She cried out, her body jolting forward against the mattress. A thin welt appeared instantly, deep crimson and beautifully raw.

"Ten," she choked out, her voice shaking.

I recoiled my arm back again, readying for the next stroke. The belt wasn't my most brutal instrument—far from it. The thick wooden paddle I'd used on Jonny during demo night had left perfectly raised welts shaped like the etched word slut. He'd be sore for days, glowing with pride every time he felt it.

But this was her first time, her first real taste of what it meant to be mine.

And I would ease her into my need for her pain.

The second strike landed lower, just across the under-curve of her ass. She yelped, the sound slicing through the silence like music. My body hummed with it.

"Nine," she whimpered, her voice trembling but still obedient.

"Good girl," I murmured under my breath. I ran my hand across the welted flesh, feeling the raised heat beneath my fingertips. She was shaking, not from fear, but from need. I could feel it rolling off her, soaking the air between us.

The third lash came harder. She flinched, her knuckles white as she clutched the edge of the bed.

"Eight." Followed by a choked gasp.

I smiled. Each number was a surrender. Each cry was a confession of her desire.

The belt snapped again—clean, sharp.

"Seven," she hissed, breathless.

Her skin rippled beneath the leather, reddening in waves. My hand trembled, just slightly, not from uncertainty, but from restraint. I wanted more. I wanted to watch her break and rebuild under me, piece by beautiful piece.

I raised the belt once more and let it fall with a loud crack across her right cheek.

"Six!" Her voice cracked on that one, and I saw it. The tear finally escaping down her flushed cheek, landing silently on the sheets.

There it was. The crack in her walls. The first.

I leaned in, one hand pressed gently to her lower back, grounding her. "You're doing so well, pet. Just a few more. Let go for me. Let it all out."

I needed her tears, not because I wanted her broken, but because I needed to know she could handle the pain even from me. That she would trust me with her darkest truths and still beg for more.

I struck her with the belt again.

"Five!" she sobbed.

God, the sound of it. The truth in it. I felt drunk on it.

I let the belt hang loose in my grip, the leather humming with energy as I gave her the next stroke, this time with more force, letting the sound echo through the room.

"Four!" she cried out, her voice cracking fully now.

Her thighs trembled. Her hands slid an inch on the bedding, searching for stability. I could hear her sniffle, and that soft broken sound lodged itself in my chest, tightening something that always threatened to come loose when I got too close, too deep.

I couldn't stop. Not when I needed to make my point.

The fifth blow landed just across the top of the thigh, where the curve met her ass cheek. A sob tore from her lips, ragged and desperate.

"Three," she whimpered, barely audible.

I dropped the belt beside us for a moment, just long enough to run my palm down her back. Her skin was damp with sweat, her hair clinging to her cheek. Her shoulders shook with the weight of everything she was trying to hold in.

"Let it out, pet," I said softly. "This is your space. This is your freedom."

Then I lifted the belt again and brought it down, cleaner this time. Her scream was sharp, raw, too real to be faked.

"Two!" Her voice collapsed under the word, unraveling into an ugly, gasping sob.

That was it, the moment she cracked open fully.

I let the final strike land with slow precision. Not hard. Not cruel. Just enough to mark the end of this.

"One..." she whispered, and then she crumpled forward.

Her body slumped over the edge of the bed, and the sobs came, loud and racking, her breath hitching and catching in her chest like it didn't know how to move anymore. I dropped to my knees beside her, letting the belt fall away.

"Shhh," I whispered, brushing hair from her face. "You did it. It's done. You're safe."

She curled into herself, her hands clutching the sheets like she might fall off the earth if she didn't hold on tight. Her cries broke something in me, and healed something else all at once.

I wrapped my arms around her waist and pressed my cheek to her hip. "I've got you. All of you, always."

And I meant it. Every trembling, sobbing piece of her.

162

MARIANNE

Chapter 27

My breath came in ragged gasps, each one scraping through my throat like it had to fight to be let out. My face was damp with tears—hot and endless—and my hands clung to the bedding as if it were the only solid thing left in the world.

The pain still bloomed across my backside, a deep, aching fire, but the tears weren't from that alone. It was something deeper. Something older. The weight of everything I'd ever tried to hold in, all the obedience, all the shame, all the words I wasn't allowed to say. It all poured out of me in great, shuddering waves.

And through it all… she held me.

Domina's arms wrapped around my waist, her head pressed gently to my hip, her presence grounding me in a way that no one ever had. She didn't speak, didn't move to stop my sobbing. She just stayed there, letting me feel it. Letting me be this undone thing in her hands.

When the crying finally slowed, when the sobs turned into soft hiccups and shaking exhales, something else began to stir in me, something terrifying in how familiar it felt.

Need.

Not the desperate kind from fear or loneliness. This was different. This was hunger. My body ached in more ways than one, but beneath the soreness and the fatigue was a pulse of raw, undeniable desire.

I needed her.

Not just her punishment. Her touch. Her tenderness. Her mouth. Her hands.

I wanted her wrapped around me again, not to restrain me, but to hold me down and make me feel good. To fill the emptiness that the tears had carved out of me. I wanted to be touched, loved, used—*claimed*—all over again.

As if she could read my mind, she stood and pulled me into her arms. Without a word, she carried me to the shower I hadn't realized was still running. The steam was gone, the water now lukewarm, but I barely noticed. She placed me under the spray with gentle, deliberate movements, letting me rest back against the cool tile.

She stepped away.

A whimper escaped my throat before I could stop it. I didn't want to be alone, not now. I needed her. I needed more of her than I ever had before.

I didn't hear her return over the rush of the water, but I felt her and the familiar press of her hand around my waist. Then the warmth of her body as she stepped in behind me, the bare curves of her breasts pressing against my back. I shivered as she kissed up my arm, soft and reverent, trailing upward to the slope of my shoulder and the curve of my neck.

Her other arm slid around my front, and her hand grasped my left breast, squeezing gently. I let out a soft moan, leaning into her touch, my body aching for more, aching for her.

She explored my body with a soft, sensual teasing, her right hand drawing slow, deliberate circles along my hip bone before dipping lower, hovering just above where I ached for her. Her left hand pinched my hardened nipple, sending a sharp spark of pleasure through me.

I leaned back into her, my body flush against hers, craving every inch of contact. That's when I felt it, the soft, firm length pressing against my sore backside, a lingering reminder of my earlier punishment. And fuck, the thrill it sparked in me was instant. My mind raced to the only possible conclusion.

I reached back, fingers grazing along her hip, and there it was— the rough texture of a strap digging lightly into her skin.

A breathy, desperate moan escaped me. "Domina..."

"Find something you like, pet?" she murmured, her voice thick with amusement and promise, the wicked smile practically dripping from her words.

Her fingers toyed with my clit, light and maddening, and I shuddered beneath her touch. I ran my hand along her side, urging her on, needing more. She responded by squeezing my breast harder, sending another jolt of sensation through me.

My left hand reached for hers, fingers dancing up the taut lines of her arm. I closed my eyes, letting the sensations consume me— the warm water cascading over my body, the heat of her breath against my neck, the electric pleasure of her touch, the smooth slide of her skin against mine, and the firm press of her silicone cock nudging the sore ache of my ass.

It was too much and not nearly enough.

"Please," I whimpered, the word trembling from my lips.

With that, she braced me against the tiled wall, lifting my right leg to rest on the small corner shelf. Her right hand supported my thigh, while her other slipped away from my breast, leaving me clinging to the slick wall for balance.

I felt the firm head of her cock slide through my folds, teasing my clit with deliberate, slick strokes. I felt her find my entrance and press against it, steady and patient. The sensation of her filling me full, drew a sharp breath from me.

I had never been fucked before. Not really. Everything I'd ever done, every touch, every sensation, it had only ever been for her, for my Domina. And now, every moment with her was something new, something thrilling and overwhelming. Each experience filled a need I hadn't even known existed.

She began to move faster, her rhythm deepening. Each thrust sent a jolt of sensation through my core, pleasure coiling tighter with every stroke. My hands slipped along the wet tile as I tried to hold myself up, to stay open for her, but my legs trembled beneath me.

"That's it," she whispered, her voice a low growl of approval. "Take it all, pet."

I moaned, the sound raw and desperate. Her hand snaked around my waist, holding me steady, grounding me, while her other slid down between my thighs. Her fingers found my clit again and circled it in perfect, tormenting strokes. The pressure was unbearable. Perfect.

"Domina... I can't—" I cried out, my voice cracking.

"Yes, you can," she purred, nipping the curve of my shoulder. "You'll come for me. You'll fall apart for me."

I shattered.

The orgasm ripped through me, sharp and all-consuming. My body shook violently and I cried out, her name breaking from my lips like a prayer. "Domina" I clenched around her, waves of pleasure crashing over me again and again as my thighs trembled and my muscles gave way.

She held me through it all, never letting me fall.

Even as I sagged against the wall, breathless and spent, she stayed inside me a moment longer, letting me feel the full weight of her dominance, the warmth of her body pressed against mine. I whimpered softly, not from pain or fear, but from something deeper. From need, vulnerability. The ache of being completely known.

Then, she eased out of me, careful and slow.

Her hands were suddenly everywhere. Steadying my leg, holding my waist, brushing damp strands of hair from my cheek. I leaned back into her chest, my legs no longer strong enough to support me. She kissed my shoulder once, then twice, before wrapping her arms around me.

"Good girl," she murmured against my ear. "So perfect. So mine."

I melted at those words.

The water still poured over us, steam clouding the small space around our bodies. My head dropped to her shoulder, eyes fluttering closed. I could feel her heartbeat against my back, slow and steady now, anchoring me in a moment that felt more real than anything else I'd ever known.

And as she turned off the water and wrapped me in a towel, scooping me into her arms like I weighed nothing, I didn't care where this all led. I only knew one truth.

I would no longer pray for repentance because if this, if she was what sent me to hell, then I no longer wanted to strive for heaven. I would rather burn.

DOMINA

Chapter 28

I wrapped her in a thick, warmed towel, the soft terry cloth clinging to her flushed skin. She trembled, not from the cold, but from everything I'd just put her through. My hand, still damp, threaded through her hair gently, after I sat her on the edge of the bed, the one I had bent her over just moments before. She looked dazed, beautiful, and completely undone. Mine.

I knelt in front of her, drying her legs with slow, careful strokes. Not because she couldn't do it herself, but because I needed to. Because if I didn't pour care back into her, I'd drown in the weight of what I'd taken.

The glow of dominance had begun to recede, like a tide pulling back. In its place came something heavier, more vulnerable, an ache I never admitted. It scared me how deeply I wanted her, not just her obedience or her body, but something more dangerous: her trust. Her affection. Her need for me.

She leaned against my shoulder, and I wrapped my arms around her, anchoring her to me. Her breath was shallow, her body soft and pliant, and I could feel her heartbeat through her skin.

"I've got you, pet," I whispered, kissing the crown of her head.

I always told myself I didn't need anyone to stay. That I wouldn't let them in until they chose to stay and proved that they would. Maybe I pushed so hard that I pushed them away. But this one? Marianne? She was burrowing in deep, infecting me with a hope I hadn't felt in years.

My hand moved in lazy strokes down her back, her damp hair clinging to my chest. This wasn't just aftercare, it was admission. A silent confession that I wanted more from her than any submissive I'd claimed before. I wanted her to see me.

I exhaled slowly and rested my chin on top of her head. She didn't ask for anything, didn't speak, and yet her silence screamed of trust.

And I didn't know why that terrified me.

Part of me wanted to tell her everything, show her all of me, bare and unfiltered. To trust her completely, the way she had trusted me. But the fear crept in, silent and insidious. The anxiety of her abandoning me wrapped around my ribs like a vice, and I shut it down.

No. It was too much, too soon.

I couldn't... Could I?

I laid her down and unbuckled the straps, letting the strap-on fall to the floor. After drying myself off, I slipped into bed beside her, wrapping my arms tightly around her. She curled into me, and I into her.

She stayed curled against me, her breath evening out as sleep finally claimed her. I didn't move for a long while, not until I was sure she had truly drifted off. I brushed a strand of damp hair from her cheek and let my lips linger against her forehead. Then, with painstaking care, I slipped from the bed and pulled the quilt higher around her body.

I left quietly, locking the door behind me with practiced ease. The click echoed in the silence of the hall. A part of me hated the sound. It wasn't supposed to be like this forever.

I padded barefoot to my bedroom and got dressed in black leggings, a soft tank, hair up. Simple. Domestic. I made my way into the kitchen and began prepping the rest of the day's meals. It was Saturday, which meant more structure, more rituals. Comfort through routine. The scent of garlic and onion filled the air as I diced, stirred, sautéed, but my mind wasn't on the food.

I couldn't keep her locked in the basement forever. That had never been the plan, not truly. The space below had been meant as a sanctuary, as a place to transition. To shed what had been done to her, to find who she could become. But eventually, she'd need more than a locked door and whispered praises. She'd need the real world again. Or... our version of it.

I stirred the sauce harder than necessary, the spoon clattering against the edge of the pot.

I didn't want to lose her, but I wouldn't cage her either. That wasn't the kind of Dominant I wanted to be. She wasn't just a pet I wanted to keep locked away and fed on a schedule. She was more than that now.

I'd give her the choice. Maybe not today, maybe not tomorrow. But I would. Because if she stayed, it had to be her decision. Entirely.

But first... I had to give her something worth choosing.

I wiped my hands on a kitchen towel and leaned against the counter, staring into the pot of simmering sauce like it might offer answers. My stomach twisted, not from hunger, but from something deeper, an ache I couldn't quite name.

This wasn't like the others. She wasn't like the others.

With them, I could compartmentalize. I could guide them through obedience and submission with the firm hand of protocol and routine. But with Marianne, everything felt blurred. Her eyes cracked something open in me that I had spent years sealing shut. The way she looked at me, like I was her anchor, her goddamn salvation, and it was intoxicating and terrifying.

173

Structure. I needed structure. If I didn't define the boundaries now, everything would unravel.

I moved to the drawer near the coffee pot, where I kept spare notebooks. Grabbing a pen, I flipped open to a blank page and began to write.

House Protocol – Marianne (Pet)

If she was going to live outside the basement, if I was going to let her into my real world, there needed to be rules. A contract of sorts. Not formal, not signed in blood... but clear. Unshakeable.

RULES:

1. Respect and address me only as Domina when we are alone or in a scene.

2. Always ask for permission before touching me or yourself in any sexual capacity.

3. Maintain your physical health—three meals a day, water, hygiene. I care for your body, and so will you.

4. You do not lie to me. Ever.

If you disobey, disrespect, or break these rules, you will be punished appropriately. Depending on the severity, you may be returned to the basement and placed under restricted protocol.

I stared at the words, rereading them twice, I decided I would need to refine this to make it perfect, for her. Even so, my handwriting was steady. The rules were familiar. Comfortable. This was how I kept control. This was how I'd protect both of us from losing our way.

She would accept these. I was sure of it.

And if she didn't?

I clenched the pen until my knuckles ached. Then she wasn't ready for what we were building. And I'd lock the door again because I couldn't, no, wouldn't, let feelings derail what we needed most: obedience, trust, safety, control.

For Fucks sake, part of me already wanted to punish her again. Part of me wanted to give her the world.

And that's exactly why I had to do this.

MARIANNE

Chapter 29

I woke to the soft creak of silence, the kind that felt thick, like the walls were holding their breath.

The bed was still warm beneath me, the sheets lightly scented with Domina's skin, but she was gone. I sat up slowly, my body sore in the best, most confusing ways. My inner thighs ached, my ass throbbed with each subtle shift, and my lips… they still tingled from her kiss.

It wasn't until I swung my legs over the edge of the bed that I noticed the tray.

A wooden tray sat neatly on the small table across the room, holding a glass of water, a plate of noodles topped with rich red tomato sauce fragrant with garlic and onion, a slice of buttered toast, and a small bowl of ripe strawberries. Beside it lay a folded piece of cream-colored parchment, weighted down with a smooth black stone.

Beside the table, a soft, simple dress had been draped over the back of a wooden chair. Linen, maybe. Pale blue, with thin straps and a long flowing skirt. Modest, but beautiful. Comfortable. I ran my fingers across the fabric like it might disappear if I wasn't careful.

I picked up the note and unfolded it.

Pet,

Eat. Drink all the water. Put on the dress.

Then sit and memorize the following rules. You will not be quizzed, yet, but you will be expected to follow them without hesitation. They are for your safety, your clarity, and your pleasure.

This is not a punishment.

This is your beginning.

—D

My hands trembled slightly as I flipped the page and read what followed. Each line was deliberate. Controlled. Not cruel. No, never cruel, but commanding in a way that made my stomach twist with both fear and excitement. She wanted me to learn. To obey. To belong. To her.

I set the page down with a deep breath and reached for the dress, slipping it over my head, the fabric soft and comforting. I obeyed, not just because she said so but because I wanted to please her. Because somewhere deep down, being given direction felt like safety.

And maybe... love.

My heart pounded a little as I sat down and picked up the note again. I began to commit the words to memory, the rules. Expectations. Structure.

God help me, I felt something inside me relax.

This... made sense. Rules I could follow. Expectations I could meet. There were no confusing grey areas here. No disappointed looks across the dinner table because I didn't iron the hem just right. No Bible verses weaponized to make me smaller. No constant guessing what version of my mother or father would be waiting for me when I walked in the door.

Just clear boundaries. Clear rewards. Clear consequences.

I swallowed hard, my throat suddenly tight with emotion. Was it strange that this didn't feel like captivity? That it felt... like freedom?

I felt seen here.

Useful. Wanted. Cherished.

Like I had a purpose beyond what I could clean or who I could please. And in her arms, for the first time in my life, I didn't feel wrong.

But then the thoughts came crawling in like they always did.

What if this is just another prison? A prettier one. A warmer one. But a cage all the same.

I pressed my palms to my eyes. The guilt still clung to me like a second skin. Guilt for feeling happy. Guilt for craving her touch, her voice, her praise. Guilt for obeying so quickly, so easily. For calling her Domina and meaning it with every fiber of my being.

Maybe I had replaced one form of obedience with another. Maybe I was just trading one form of control for a darker kind.

But then why… Why did I feel lighter here?

Why did I feel like I belonged?

And was it really so wrong to feel joy, even if it came wrapped in leather and dominance?

I looked down at the list of rules again, reading them more carefully this time, each word landing like a stone in a quiet pond.

I didn't know where this path would lead.

But I knew I wasn't ready to leave it just yet.

I set the note back on the table and took a small sip of the water. Cool. Clean. It grounded me just enough for the tremble in my hands to ease.

But my thoughts didn't quiet.

They wandered back to where I once called home and back to the church.

I pictured the narrow hallways of New Hope Community, the way the sanctuary lights buzzed overhead while the choir sang of righteousness and obedience. I could hear my mother's sharp whispers behind me, telling me to sit straighter, smile wider, "Be a good example."

The memory clung like old perfume, sickly sweet and impossible to wash off.

Back then, I thought goodness meant silence. Meekness. That denying yourself desire was a form of purity. I believed that being "chosen" meant never questioning, never wanting, and certainly never *feeling* what I felt now.

How could I go back to that?

How could I return to a life where my body was an inconvenience and my thoughts a sin?

Here, in this place, with her, I wasn't a burden or a project. I was cherished. I was praised. I was broken open and still seen as whole. Even in this chaos, even in this strange, dark dynamic, there was more care than I'd ever been offered in that house. In that church.

And if I left now… if I tried to return to my old life…

Would I even survive it?

I didn't know if I had it in me to sit through another sermon on submission; not *true* submission, but something closer to subservience. They didn't want devotion; they wanted blind obedience. To smile politely at men who stared too long and dared to call it *godly interest*. To sit quietly while my parents spoke of arranged dinners and good Christian husbands, all while I screamed silently inside.

Here, my screaming had been heard. It had been *answered*.

I curled my legs beneath me and clutched the soft cotton of the dress she'd left for me. My fingers tightened around the fabric as hot tears welled in my eyes.

I didn't know what I was becoming here.

Though I knew what I wasn't anymore.

I wasn't their good little christian girl.

I never would be again.

DOMINA

Chapter 30

What the fuck am I doing? God. Okay, I can do this.

I pulled the key from around my neck, my hand trembling as I lifted it toward the door. I had waited, which had given her the rest of the day and the entire night. I'd given her space, time to process, time to read and memorize the rules, *my rules*, before bringing her out of the basement. My dungeon. My sanctuary.

But now it was morning. Sunday morning. And I was about to trust her more than I ever had with any of the others.

The others had never gotten this far. They were made to earn it— and the first time I let them out, they ran. Every single one of them. And I had… I had made the choices I had to make.

The lock clicked as I turned the key and opened the heavy door.

And then I forgot how to breathe.

She was sitting on the edge of the bed in that thin cotton slip I had left for her. Her nipples peaked through the fabric, her lips soft and flushed, her eyes locked on mine.

She was utterly breathtaking.

Mine.

She didn't speak. She didn't need to. Her eyes followed me like I was gravity itself, and maybe I was. I stepped fully into the room, closing the door behind me with a soft but final click. The sound echoed.

"Good morning, pet," I said, keeping my voice low and measured, though my pulse was anything but calm.

She nodded, eyes still wide and waiting. Her fingers were curled together in her lap, nervous but obedient.

I crossed the room slowly, savoring the way her breath hitched the closer I came. When I reached her, I stood just inches away and let the silence stretch between us like a drawn wire.

"You read the rules?" My voice stern despite my nerves, which I didn't understand. I had done this many times before, maybe too many. I wanted to hear the rules. I had reworked them several times before I fully decided on the final seven, and they were perfect.

"Yes, Domina," she said, soft and breathy. Her voice was stronger than yesterday, but still dipped in reverence.

I brushed a strand of hair from her cheek, letting my knuckles trail down her jawline. "Recite them for me, pet. Word for word."

She swallowed, visibly gathering herself.

"One," she began, her voice trembling slightly but steadying as she continued. "I belong to Domina. My body, my mind, and my pleasure are hers to guide and shape."

"Good." I nodded, and sat down on the edge of the bed beside her, close but not touching. "Keep going."

"Two. I will obey without hesitation unless given permission to question or speak freely." Her voice quivered slightly.

"Three. I will be honest with Domina at all times. Lies, omissions, or manipulation will result in punishment." I watched her, the way her shoulders squared with each line, how the shift in her voice revealed just how seriously she had taken this.

"Four. If I break a rule or act out of line, I will be punished. Punishment is not cruelty…it is care. It is structure." Her voice cracked slightly on that line, and I placed a hand on her knee, grounding her.

"Five. I will not leave the house without Domina's permission. If I try, I will be returned to the basement for further training." I watched her worry her bottom lip between her teeth for a moment.

"Six. My pleasure is a privilege, not a right. It will be given and taken as Domina sees fit." She paused, closing her eyes and breathing deeply before finishing. "Seven. I will eat, drink, rest, and care for my body as instructed, because this body belongs to Domina, and she will not let me waste it."

I let the silence settle again as I let those words linger in the air between us.

"Perfect," I whispered. "You make me proud, pet."

She exhaled as though she had been holding her breath the whole time. I leaned in and kissed her cheek, soft, restrained. I whispered, "Stand."

She did, rising slowly but without hesitation.

"Today, you'll come upstairs. You've earned breakfast out of this room. But," I said, tilting her chin to meet my gaze. "You'll be naked. The dress is only for if I tell you to put it on. Understood?"

"Yes, Domina." She grew flush as her eyes looked to the ground.

"Good girl. Now come. Walk a step behind me. Quietly." And with that, I led her out of the basement, up into the morning light.

The stairs creaked under our steps, her bare feet whispering behind the sound of my boots. I didn't look back, I didn't need to. I could feel her presence, that delicious mix of hesitation and devotion radiating like heat behind me.

The kitchen greeted us with warm sun streaming through the small window over the sink. It was modest; stone countertops, hanging copper pans, a small herb garden blooming in the windowsill. The smell of strong coffee and cinnamon still hung in the air.

I had prepared everything before going downstairs—oatmeal with brown sugar and butter, crisp slices of bacon, and toast slathered in honey butter. Two cups of coffee steamed on the table, one already mixed with her favorite amount of sugar and cream.

I turned to her once we stepped into the room. She stood at attention, hands behind her back, eyes lowered.

I smiled, pride blooming low in my chest. "Come sit, pet."

She moved quickly but with grace, settling into the chair I had pulled out for her. Her thighs pressed together, self-conscious, but she didn't try to hide.

I sat across from her, placing my napkin in my lap and lifting my coffee. "You've earned this moment. Don't ruin it by fidgeting."

She stilled instantly, shoulders squaring.

I watched her closely as she took her first bite. Her eyelids fluttered at the taste, and a soft moan slipped past her lips before she could stop it.

I chuckled. "Careful, pet. That kind of sound earns attention."

Her face flushed crimson. "Yes, Domina."

We ate in silence for a few minutes, the only sounds the clink of cutlery and the occasional contented sigh. I allowed her to enjoy the food uninterrupted. She needed this—structure, reward, the grounding of being seen and cared for. Though, I needed it too.

As she sipped her coffee, she glanced up at me through her lashes. "Domina?"

I raised a brow. "Speak."

"Thank you… for trusting me." Her voice was sweet and lovely.

Those words hit harder than I expected. I placed my cup down carefully and studied her. The bruises from the belt were faintly visible on her thighs, and the red marks from my handprints still lingered on her skin like a signature.

"Don't make me regret it," I said softly.

She didn't flinch. "I won't."

I let my gaze drift over her plush, beautiful body as she sat there, sipping her coffee. A ravenous hunger twisted in my chest. New, wonderful, and terrible all at once. I studied every curve, every ripple, every little quiver in her as she drank, savoring the view and the moment.

"Pet, come here." My voice was full of need.

I stood, and she obeyed with soft, quiet movements. I gripped her sore ass firmly with both hands as I pulled her against me, only the fabric of my clothes between us. The soft, breathy whimper that escaped her lips fueled the fire already smoldering in my core.

Without hesitation, I lifted her and set her ass on the edge of the table. She let out a surprised squeak, and I couldn't help but grin at the sound.

"Place your hands on the table behind your back, pet. And don't move them," I commanded with practiced ease.

She obeyed, her back arching just enough to thrust her chest forward, her nipples tightening to taut peaks. The sight made my breath catch.

I spread her legs wide, stepping between them as I pulled a chair in close and sat down. My fingers trailed slowly up the creamy expanse of her thighs, exploring every lush curve like a treasure I intended to claim.

She was breathtaking like this. Open, obedient, and trembling with anticipation. Her breath quickened as my fingers danced higher, teasing just along the crease where her thigh met the soaked heat between her legs.

"You're already wet for me, pet," I murmured, my voice low and indulgent. "Do you even realize how perfect you look like this?"

Her lips parted, but she didn't speak. Good. She was learning.

I let my fingertips ghost over her inner thigh without touching the place she needed me most. She squirmed just slightly, her muscles tensing, her nipples pebbled with want. I leaned in, inhaling the scent of her arousal. It was sweet, warm, and utterly intoxicating.

My breath fanned against her clit without touching it. Her hips jerked.

"Don't move." I spoke the words as I grinned wickedly.

Her fingers gripped at the table tighter, knuckles white with restraint. My smirk only grew.

I placed one hand on her belly, firm and grounding, while the other finally slid up, barely brushing the slickness of her pussy. She gasped, her head falling back, a soft moan slipping from her throat.

"Such a good girl," I whispered, tracing slow, deliberate circles around her clit. "But you haven't earned more yet. Let me hear you ask nicely."

Her thighs trembled, her body practically begging me. "Please, Domina." Her words were soft and breathy. In that moment I knew I wouldn't be able to resist her.

"That's right. Now you will be my dessert," I said, my lips brushing the sensitive skin at the top of her thigh. "And, you're going to sit here and learn what it means to be worshipped."

I held her open and let my tongue begin its slow, thorough devotion.

MARIANNE

Chapter 31

My breath caught in my throat the second her fingers grazed my skin. The gentleness in her touch was a lie. It only masked the storm I knew she could unleash at any second. I was spread open on the table, trembling, her mouth so close I could feel the heat of her breath but not the relief of her lips.

Every nerve in my body screamed for more.

She hadn't even truly touched me yet, and I was already spiraling, my thighs quaking, my fingers clutching at the table like it was the only thing keeping me tethered to earth. My hands ached from the tension, but I didn't dare move. I wouldn't disobey her. Not now, not when I needed her like I needed air.

I heard her murmur something about worship, and the word echoed in my chest like a church bell, shaking loose something buried deep inside me. Was that what this was? Worship? I had only ever known devotion as something expected, demanded, never something that *felt* like this. Never something that set me on fire from the inside out.

And then her tongue touched me.

I gasped, too loud and too needy, but I couldn't stop the sound. My hips jolted, every muscle tightening. She held me down with one strong hand on my stomach, keeping me in place while her mouth moved slowly, deliberately, like she was learning the shape of my desire with every flick and swirl of her tongue.

I couldn't think. I could barely breathe. The shame that usually crept in during these moments, the voices in my head, my mother's words, the weight of purity and sin. None of it mattered. None of it could survive her touch.

I whimpered. I begged. I forgot every rule except the one that mattered: *keep my hands behind my back and stay still.* My legs were shaking so badly I didn't know how much longer I could last.

"Please," I whispered, barely able to form the word. "Please, Domina..."

She didn't stop. She only hummed against me, the vibration sent lightning straight through me.

Tears burned at the corners of my eyes, not from pain, but from the overwhelming *rightness* of it. How could something so forbidden feel so holy?

And still, she didn't let me fall.

God, I was hers. I was becoming utterly, shamelessly, wrecked by her.

I gritted my teeth against the moan that threatened to tear from my throat. My hands ached from how tightly I clenched the table behind me, my knuckles white, nails digging into wood. Her mouth was still on me—slow, steady, devastating. She didn't rush. She didn't relent. She knew what she was doing to me.

I could feel the pulse of my heartbeat between my thighs, a deep throb that grew more insistent with every flick of her tongue, every purposeful pause, every maddening swirl that just barely avoided the one spot I needed her to touch most.

It was agony. It was ecstasy.

She pressed her hand firmer against my stomach when my hips tried to rise to meet her mouth. I cried out, a strangled sound that slipped from my lips despite everything, and her nails grazed my skin, not hard, just enough to warn.

"Be still, pet," she murmured against me, her voice a low vibration that made me shudder. "You'll come when I say you can."

A fresh wave of heat flooded me at her words, my body traitorous and wild, responding with reckless abandon. I bit my lip so hard it almost bled, trying to ground myself in the pain, in the control, in her. I was floating—no, falling—and the only thing anchoring me was her voice, her breath, her body.

My eyes fluttered closed, but not before I caught her looking up at me, her gaze dark and burning. It wasn't just desire. It was something deeper. Something possessive. Protective. Predatory.

I wanted to drown in it.

And yet she pulled back, just a breath, just enough to make me feel the loss of her touch like a slap. My whole body strained forward, desperate, aching, and she only chuckled, low and cruel.

"You want it so badly, don't you, pet?" she said softly, her fingers grazing the inside of my thigh, just enough to make my skin prickle and twitch.

I nodded frantically, chest heaving, legs trembling.

She didn't touch me again. Instead she let the silence stretch, let the ache swell inside me like a storm cloud ready to burst.

"I think," she said, brushing her lips against the top of my thigh. "You need to learn how to wait for me."

I whimpered. My whole body ached with denial, with need, with the unbearable anticipation of her next move.

And still, I didn't move. I waited. For her.

My thighs trembled with the effort it took to stay still, to obey. Every inch of me buzzed with need, my skin alive and desperate for her touch. I couldn't breathe right, each inhale shallow, every exhale ragged. My chest rose and fell like I'd run a mile, but I hadn't moved at all.

She hovered between my legs like a shadow just out of reach, her breath ghosting across my slick skin. I could feel the humidity of her closeness. The maddening *almost* of it.

"Good," she whispered, the single word curling around my spine like smoke. "Obedience looks utterly beautiful on you."

Her praise made something inside me tighten, coil, and I felt the wetness between my thighs slick further. My back arched, but I caught myself—*barely*. My palms pressed harder into the table behind me, anchoring me there, shaking.

She didn't need to bind me. Her words did it just fine.

Domina's hand trailed up my thigh, soft at first, then firmer, her fingers pressing into the soft flesh like she was marking it. Not bruising. However, the promise was there that she wanted to claim me.

A whine escaped me, it was pitiful, needy, begging without words.

She chuckled, the sound sending a fresh wave of fire crashing through me. I was unraveling. She was *letting* me unravel. Slowly. Deliberately. With a twisted kind of tenderness that I didn't know how to handle.

Her mouth was *right* there.

So close I could feel the heat of it. My clit throbbed, desperate for just the *slightest* friction.

And still… nothing.

"Do you feel it?" she asked softly. "That ache? That ache is mine."

I whimpered again, nodding, my whole body trembling now with restraint. She pressed a kiss to the inside of my knee. Then another, higher this time. Then a third. It was agonizingly slow, just where my thigh met my pelvis.

My breath hitched.

But her lips never touched where I needed them.

Instead, her hand lifted. She gently, so *gently*, ran a single fingertip along my soaked slit, but not over my throbbing clit. Up and down but never over the one spot I wanted, *needed* it. My hips jerked in betrayal, but she pressed down again on my stomach.

"No," she said, firmer. "Still."

I stilled. I could feel tears prick at the corners of my eyes, not from pain. Not even from frustration. From being *seen*. From being held like this, in this terrible, beautiful in-between. On display. On edge. Owned.

Yet, I wanted more. God help me, I never wanted her to stop.

She finally moved.

Her mouth replaced her hand, and I nearly screamed from the shock of contact. Her tongue slid between the contours of my center, soft, confident, and claiming. My hips bucked, but her hands clamped down, one on my stomach, the other flat against my thigh, pinning me to the table.

"Still," she growled into my skin. The vibration of her voice against my most sensitive places shattered something inside me.

I didn't just fall apart—I *exploded.*

Her tongue circled my clit, slow and relentless, building me fast and hard toward the edge I'd been balancing on since the moment she spread my legs. My arms trembled from holding myself upright. My whole body tightened, drawn taut like a bowstring.

She sucked with sharp, focused pressure, and I broke.

A cry ripped from my throat, raw and loud, and I came with a violence I didn't know I was capable of. My legs shook uncontrollably, my breath vanished, and my body spasmed around her mouth.

But she didn't stop. She held me there, prolonging the pleasure, pushing me through it. Her mouth stayed locked on me, her tongue working me through every pulse, every wave. It was too much, and not enough, and everything I had ever wanted.

Tears spilled from my eyes as my orgasm stretched longer than I thought possible. It felt like being unraveled and rebuilt, like every breath I'd ever held in my life was finally let go.

When she finally pulled away, she didn't speak. She just pressed her forehead gently to my thigh and breathed.

And I… I sobbed.

Not from pain. Not even from overstimulation. But from release. From surrender. From feeling something I had only ever imagined but never believed I could have.

She lifted her head, her lips glistening with my arousal. She looked up at me like I was something holy. Reverent.

"You're all mine, Marieanne," she whispered.

And it was everything I never knew I needed.

DOMINA

Chapter 32

The soft clack of my keyboard filled the room, a familiar rhythm that usually calmed me. But today, the cadence felt off, distracted, disrupted.

Because she was here.

Marianne lay stretched out across the bed, her golden-brown hair a tangled halo against the pillow, her skin glowing in the late morning light. She wore one of my button-down shirts, blue cotton, oversized on her soft, plush body. The hem had ridden up to expose the thick swell of her thighs and just a sliver of pink cotton between her legs.

I hadn't told her she could wear panties today, but I let it go.

Her obedience the past few days had been near perfect. She recited her rules without hesitation each morning. She followed protocol. She didn't ask to leave, didn't flinch from punishment or correction. And yet... there was something in the way she sprawled now, completely at ease, one arm slung above her head, the other resting over her belly as she hummed softly to herself.

Content. Too content?

My fingers paused over the keyboard.

Was this what I wanted? Not the control. That part was natural. It lived in me like breath and blood. No, it was *this,* the stillness. The warmth of another body near mine. The hum of someone existing freely under my roof, in my space, without tension or fear. That was the part I didn't know how to handle.

Love, if I dared call it that, was messy. And I had always kept messiness at arm's length.

She shifted and glanced my way. When our eyes met, she smiled.

It disarmed me every time.

"What are you working on?" she asked softly, voice scratchy from sleep.

"Client mock-ups," I said, my voice steadier than I felt. "Branding package for a boudoir photographer. The irony isn't lost on me."

Marianne laughed, the sound wrapping around my ribcage like silk and barbed wire.

I turned back to the screen, but I wasn't looking at the design. I was watching her reflection in the glass. The way she stretched like a cat, lazy and sensual, without meaning to. I wondered how long this balance could hold, between indulgence and structure, intimacy and distance, reality and the dark edges where we began.

She trusted me. And fuck, I didn't want to break that.

She stood quietly from the bed, the shirt falling just enough to brush the tops of her thighs, and padded over to me on bare feet. I didn't look at her, I couldn't. Not when my chest was already tightening with something too gentle, too tender.

She slipped her arms around my shoulders from behind and pressed her cheek against the side of my head. Soft. Warm. Familiar.

Her weight leaned just enough to settle against me, like we had done this a hundred times. As if we were just... a couple. As if this were safe.

And for a second, I let her. Just a second.

Then, something inside me bristled. I flinched at the domestic ease, the dangerous sweetness of it. A part of me curled back into the steel spine of command.

This was not what we did. This wasn't earned yet.

I stood suddenly and she backed away, startled, eyes wide.

"Forward present." My tone cut clean and sharp through the room.

Marianne froze, the warmth in her cheeks draining to confusion, then flushed red with realization. She dropped her gaze, her breath catching.

"Yes, Domina," she whispered, instantly shifting.

She faced me, feet shoulder-width apart, arms lifted, hands cupped beneath her breasts. Her nipples peaked against the thin shirt. I didn't let my eyes linger, instead I looked beyond her.

"Recite your rules. Now." Anger tinted my tone as I gave the command.

She swallowed. "One, I belong to Domina. My body, my mind, and my pleasure are hers to guide and shape.

Two. I will obey without hesitation unless given permission to question or speak freely.

Three. I will be honest with Domina at all times. Lies, omissions, or manipulation will result in punishment.

Four. If I break a rule or act out of line, I will be punished. Punishment is not cruelty…it is care. It is structure.

Five. I will not leave the house without Domina's permission. If I try, I will be returned to the basement for further training.

Six. My pleasure is a privilege, not a right. It will be given and taken as Domina sees fit.

Seven. I will eat, drink, rest, and care for my body as instructed, because this body belongs to Domina, and she will not let me waste it."

I stepped closer, close enough to see the shiver that danced across her arms. Her lips were trembling slightly. Not from fear. No, she knew better by now, but from shame at overstepping. From the sharp reminder that my control had boundaries, and she had brushed too close to one.

"Good girl," I murmured, cupping her chin between my fingers. "But don't confuse tenderness for weakness, pet. I gave you comfort because you earned it. That doesn't mean you get to take what hasn't been offered."

"Yes, Domina." Her voice was softer now, breathless. Penitent.

I watched her chest rise and fall, the fight between desire and discipline visible in every line of her body.

"Now," I said, stepping back. "Get on your knees and stay there until I finish this design. Then we'll see if you've remembered how to ask for affection properly."

She dropped to her knees without protest, folding her hands neatly behind her back. Her eyes stayed down, her breath controlled, but I saw it in her posture. The ache for correction, for direction. For me.

I sat again in my chair, pulled my wacom drawing tab in front of me, and returned to the half-finished design glowing on the monitor. The muted blue tones were too soft. I needed something bolder, sharper, like the pressure coiled just under my skin.

I traced a line with my stylus. Smooth curve. Precision.

But my mind wasn't on the commission anymore.

She had touched me like a lover. Not a submissive. Not my pet. As though the line between us were hers to blur.

My jaw clenched.

I gave her structure, purpose, devotion she'd never tasted in that empty house of hers. I pulled her from hell, and still a part of her reached out to make this soft.

I switched to a bolder brush, dragged it hard through the stroke. The composition snapped into place. It was cleaner this way. *Stronger.* Like I had to be.

I glanced down. She remained motionless. Obedient. Her knees spread perfectly, her spine straight despite the concrete beneath her. Her shoulders trembled faintly from the weight of my silence. Good.

I finished the final adjustment on the mockup, saved the file, and closed the laptop.

I stood.

She flinched, not visibly, not shamefully, but with that subtle, delicious tension that told me she knew what was coming.

I walked past her to my closet and opened the door to where I kept the implements for moments like this. Not punishment out of anger, but *discipline*. To reinforce our dynamic. To protect it.

To protect me.

I selected the thin cane, the one that sang when it sliced the air. I didn't need bruises. I needed *memory*. I needed her to remember who I was and who she had agreed to be.

I turned to face her again. Her breath hitched.

I didn't speak right away. I let the silence sink in. Let her squirm in her own thoughts.

She had wrapped her arms around me like we were equals.

I circled her slowly, running the cane gently along her shoulder as I passed behind her. She exhaled a shaky breath but didn't move.

I spoke finally, low and calm. "You forgot your place, pet."

"Yes, Domina," she whispered.

"Do you understand why this is necessary?" I toyed with the cane in my hand, the long black length of it swirling in the air, the leather covered handle a grounding weight.

She paused. "Yes, Domina. Because I overstepped without permission." I let that linger between us before I stepped in front of her, lifting her chin with the cane's tip.

"Five strokes. Across your thighs. You will thank me for each. You will not flinch. You will not cry." My voice was thick with control and desire to see her back under my will.

She nodded slowly, then added, "Yes, Domina."

I guided her gently but firmly up onto her feet and positioned her against the wall, with her legs spread, arms braced, palms flat against the wall, the oversized shirt bunched up around her waist.

Each stroke I landed with purpose. Sharp. Exact.

She hissed. But she didn't cry.

And after each one: "Thank you, Domina."

By the fifth, her thighs trembled. Her skin held thin red welts, temporary, but vivid. A reminder etched in warmth and sting. My desire to take her and fuck her right there against the wall consumed me. I pushed away my desire until I was only left with the dampness between my thighs.

Finally, I purred, "Good girl," against her ear.

I stepped back, breathing hard, not from the effort but the thrill of it. Not just power, but control. The restoration of balance. That is what kept me grounded.

If she was going to stay, if she was truly mine, she had to love the structure I need. As much as I craved her touch, I needed her submission more.

I let the cane drop to the floor and cupped her face in my hands.

"Now," I said, brushing my thumb across her flushed cheek. "Come kneel by my chair again. This time, you will earn the right to kiss my thighs."

MARIANNE

Chapter 33

The sting still throbbed on my thighs, an echo of each stroke, etched like a brand beneath my skin. I knelt obediently beside her chair, where she had commanded me, my posture perfect, my hands resting lightly on my thighs. I was quiet. Still. Just as she expected me to be.

And yet... my thoughts were anything but still.

Heat churned low in my belly, not just from the punishment, but from the way she had looked at me when she gave it. She hadn't just seen my body, she had seen me. I had craved every second of it, even as the cane bit into me and made me wince.

How could pain feel so much like being held?

I kept my eyes down, lashes lowered, breathing steady, but beneath the surface, I was unraveling again, in a different way. The ache inside me wasn't just for her touch now. It was for something more dangerous. Something more forbidden.

I wanted to know *her.*

Not just Domina. Not just the commands and the punishments and the ecstasy she teased me with so skillfully.

I wanted to know the woman behind all of that. The woman who hummed when she cooked, who wrote little lists in the margin of her notebook while I slept. The one whose smile cracked like lightning when she didn't think I was watching. Who tucked me in, who sometimes looked at me like she didn't believe I was real.

I risked a glance upward.

She was focused again, her dark eyes scanning the glow of the monitor as she worked, one leg tucked beneath her, her bare arm resting on the desk beside a drawing tablet. Her fingers moved with steady precision, stylus gliding across the pad in fluid strokes. Her posture was relaxed but alert, completely in control, even in her stillness.

Just along the bottom of the desk were four cube-shaped shelves tucked beneath it. In the corner of the one on the far left... something black caught my eye.

A book. Leather-bound. Old, worn. Tucked in the corner where she probably thought I wouldn't notice. No label, no markings, just a faint scratch along the spine. My breath caught.

Was it a journal?

The urge to know tugged at me like gravity. What was in there? Notes? Names? Past submissives? Secrets? Me?

I looked away quickly, fixing my gaze on the floor.

You're hers, I reminded myself. *She trusts you to obey.*

But the thought had already burrowed in. Lodged under my skin like a splinter.

Later, maybe when she was asleep. If she left it there. If I could reach it without making a sound.

I swallowed hard, guilt already prickling along the edges of my mind. But the hunger for answers was louder than my shame.

I needed to know who I was kneeling for. Who she really was... when she wasn't Domina.

The room had fallen into a quiet rhythm, the soft clacking of Domina's keyboard had slowed, the blue light of the multiple screens on the desk casting shadows across her sharp cheekbones. I watched from my place on the floor as she blinked, leaned back, and let out a long, soft sigh.

Her hand drifted to her glass of water. She took a sip, sat the tablet on the desk, and stretched with a graceful roll of her shoulders that made my breath catch for reasons I didn't fully understand.

Then, without a word, she rose from her chair and turned toward the bedroom.

I stayed perfectly still, waiting as her footsteps faded into the hallway. The distant sound of the bathroom door closing. The click of the lock.

My heart thundered in my chest.

Now.

I rose off my heels slowly, soundlessly. My legs ached from the long stretch of kneeling, but adrenaline drowned the discomfort. I crawled forward a few feet on the floor and reached the edge of the desk.

The book was heavier than I expected. The leather was cool beneath my fingers, well-worn but clearly cared for. My fingers trembled as I pulled it into the pool of lamplight and opened the first page.

Lists of rules. Rituals. Observations.

I swallowed hard as I skimmed through a dozen or more pages written in a tight, elegant hand.

Dates. Names. Descriptions.

"Tess – too soft. Broke after her first punishment. Refused aftercare. Left within the week. Lied."

Next page…

"Naomi – promising, but manipulative. Tried to top from the bottom. Left after a month. Needs harsher punishments."

I flipped the page again.

"E – never trusted me. Still hear her voice in my head. Whimpered at nothing. Returned."

Each name struck like a heartbeat in my skull.

She had done this before. Not just played with people, but kept them, and trained them. Had they all left her or did something else happen?

At the center of the book was the last filled page marked only by the current year and a name staring back at me.

"Marianne. 2005"

My breath caught. I leaned in, reading the entry beneath.

"Gentle. Starved. Believes she's broken. She begs for permission to feel. I see the fight in her. I see the ache. I see everything I've ever wanted to save. But if she leaves, I won't survive it. I'll break. It will be the end of it all. I don't want to cage her, but I don't trust her to stay without one."

The room swayed. I dropped to the floor, still gripping the book.

She didn't trust me. Not really. She thought she had to keep me locked up to keep me close. The part of me that had grown soft under her care curled into itself, stung. The other part—the darker, needier part, ached at the words *"I won't survive it."*

Was I her weakness?

And maybe… she was mine too.

A floorboard creaked down the hall. My blood ran cold.

I snapped the book shut, slid it back into place, and rushed to where I had been kneeling, settling into position just in time.

Domina returned calm and silent. Her fingers slid into my hair, her touch both tender and commanding, a quiet reassurance that I hadn't yet been found out.

My mind was still reeling. What I had read, what I had *found,* unraveled me.

The journal's words looped through my thoughts like scripture.

DOMINA

Chapter 34

I returned to the room, my pulse steady but my mind storming. I was tired and finished with work so now maybe I was ready for some play time.

I looked over and there she was, exactly as I'd left her.

Kneeling. Head bowed. Obedient.

Perfect.

My fingers slipped into her hair, combing through the soft strands. She leaned into my touch so naturally, so *eagerly,* it made something tighten low in my abdomen. I hadn't intended to break focus today, to let my discipline slip. But I was starving for her.

My restraint had limits, and she'd become my every craving.

I walked around her slowly, my hand trailing from her hair to her shoulder. She didn't flinch. Didn't look up. Her submission was total. Or at least... it appeared to be.

A flicker of doubt buzzed at the edge of my mind, but I dismissed it. She was warm and real and *mine.* I didn't want suspicion to ruin the moment.

I reached down, cupped her cheek, and tilted her face toward me.

"I need to taste you," I whispered. My voice came out lower than I expected, rougher.

I kissed her, firm and claiming. Not calculated. Not part of a scene. Just mine.

She melted into it with a soft sound that punched the breath out of my chest. I didn't want to let her go, not ever.

I broke the kiss only long enough to sit in my chair. I gave a gentle tug on her wrist.

"Up," I said, the word thick with need. "Now. Come here."

She climbed into my lap without question, her warmth pressing down into me. I adjusted her easily, one hand gripping her hip as she settled astride me.

The moment her weight sank into me, a tremor passed through both of us.

"You've earned this," I murmured, nuzzling along her jaw. "And I'm done pretending I don't want you close."

I deepened the kiss, slow and consuming as her body softened in my lap. Her lips parted for me so sweetly, so easily. God, she tasted like submission, warm and willing, tinged with the spice of earlier tears.

My fingers trailed from her jaw down the slope of her neck, ghosting over marks I'd left. Faint bruises were already beginning to form along her collarbone in the form of my fingertips, I noted absently. Then lower still, I slipped my hand between us, letting it coast over her ribs, down her waist, and around the back of her thighs.

I pressed my palm flat against her ass and dragged it slowly upward, my thumbs sliding under the hem of the pink panties, savoring the way her body tensed.

The cane welts were still warm to the touch, rising faintly beneath her skin in clean, precise lines. I traced each one with the gentleness of reverence, not apology. She whimpered softly and shifted in my lap, part ache, part want.

"Still sore?" I murmured against her lips.

She nodded against me, wordless. The way she didn't pull away, didn't hide the sound, that was what undid me.

"You wear my marks so beautifully," I whispered, and kissed the corner of her mouth. "You feel it every time you sit, don't you? A reminder that you're mine."

A shiver ran through her, and I felt her thighs tense on either side of me. I let my hand drift again, more possessive now, over her hip, across her lower back.

That's when I saw it.

Just behind her, on the lower shelf under my desk.

My pulse skipped.

My black leather journal was sitting *slightly off center*. Barely an inch. A small thing. Easy to dismiss.

Except I never left things askew.

And that notebook…

I narrowed my eyes.

I knew the way I placed my things. *Exactly* how I stacked my books. And now, that one, my private one, wasn't aligned with the rest on that shelf.

The moment twisted, pleasure snagged on suspicion.

Marianne was kissing along my throat now, and I let her. Only for a breath, two, before I pulled back.

"Pet," I said softly, tilting her chin upward. "Did you move anything today?"

She blinked at me. "No, Domina."

Her voice was soft but something about the way her breath caught just a half-beat too late made my gut twist.

Lying.

She *never* lied.

Until now.

I smiled gently. "Is that so?" I whispered.

Behind my smile a storm was building. I didn't let a flicker of suspicion show on my face. No narrowing of the eyes. No shift in tone. That wasn't how I played this game, not when something deeper was at stake.

Instead, I smiled and ran my fingers slowly through her hair, untangling a few knots from her earlier kneeling position. She leaned into the touch like a cat curling into sunlight. Trusting. Soft. Obedient.

But I no longer trusted what I was seeing.

I needed to be sure.

"Then let's see how well you remember your rules," I said lightly, like a game, like it didn't matter. I lifted her off my lap and gestured to the floor. "Kneel. Forward Present."

She dropped quickly, almost too quickly. Eager to please, or eager to hide?

Her posture was lovely, shoulders back, hands up cupping herself, tits pushed forward just the way I'd taught her. But her breathing was uneven. Not the kind brought on by arousal. No, this was tension. Anticipation. *Guilt.*

I circled her slowly, boots echoing in the room like a metronome counting down. I didn't speak. I let the silence weigh on her shoulders.

"Recite rule Three," I said softly, finally, from behind her. She inhaled, steadying herself.

"Three. I will be honest with Domina at all times. Lies, omissions, or manipulation will result in punishment."

There it was.

I watched her spine stiffen, just the slightest twitch, but I saw it. Her voice stayed smooth, too smooth, rehearsed. But I knew her too well.

Silence stretched and I heard her quick breaths and watched her squirm. One rule had already been broken.

Still, I didn't call her on it.

Instead, I stepped closer, brushing her hair back from her neck with careful fingers. I let the tension build in me, humming low behind my stern expression. Not anger, something colder. Something calculating.

"You remembered every word, pet," I praised, my voice warm, caressing. "Good girl."

She smiled, relief softening her mouth. She thought the test was over.

It wasn't.

"After breakfast," I said casually, brushing imaginary dust from her shoulder. "You'll clean my bedroom including the office. Every surface, every drawer. And I want the books under the desk dusted and restacked. Neatly. No skipping."

Her eyes twitched—just a flicker—but it was enough.

That was the shelf.

That was where I had left the journal.

Let's see what she does now. Let's see how long it takes her to crack under the weight of temptation.

Because if she does… I will know *exactly* how to deal with a curious little pet who lies.

MARIANNE

Chapter 35

I carried the cleaning supplies like a shield, hoping they would steady the war waging in my chest.

I wanted to come clean. God, I *almost* did. The weight of the journal burned behind my eyes, pressing against my conscience like a bruise I couldn't stop poking. I'd only read a few pages, but it was enough to see her in a new light. A deeper, darker light. It had shaken something loose in me.

And still… I hadn't stopped.

I *couldn't* stop.

She had given me a task to clean the bedroom and the office. Every surface. Every drawer. Including that low shelf under the desk where the journal waited, tucked beside dusty books with cracked spines and rigid silence.

I told myself I needed to understand her. That if I was going to give myself to her fully, *really* give myself, I needed to know *everything.* The rules, the punishments, the pain… They were easy to obey. But the person behind them?

That was what terrified me. And thrilled me.

I shut the door gently behind me, heart hammering so loud I feared the walls would hear it. The bedroom was dimly lit with the afternoon sun from the curtained windows, the faint scent of leather and her lingering in the air. Her desk sat like a throne against the far wall opposite the bed. It was neat, like it never touched chaos.

I took my time. Dusted the bookshelves. Wiped the desk legs. Polished the drawer handles. I even cleaned the window panes, though I knew she didn't care about smudges.

All to avoid that corner. *That shelf.*

When I finally crouched in front of it, my breath caught.

There it was, right where I'd returned it.

The black ribbon that had marked her last journal entry stuck slightly farther out than before. *She hadn't moved it.* Or so I let myself believe.

My hand trembled as I reached for it.

Just a few more lines. A few more insights. I'd be careful this time. Gentle. She wouldn't notice.

She couldn't.

I cracked the cover open slowly, cringing at every tiny sound it made. Then I read. Line after line. Thought after thought. Her handwriting sharp and elegant, each word pulsing with dominance, doubt, desire, regret. It was raw and real. And it made her *human* in a way I wasn't ready for.

But I kept going. Because I had to.

Even as I knelt on the rug, the soft bristles brushing my knees, I didn't notice how still the rest of the house had gotten.

The more I read, the colder I felt.

Not from fear, but from the weight of *knowing*.

222

Names. Dates. Initials scribbled next to entries. Sometimes a single word. The ink shifted over time, at first delicate and neat, and then, page by page, it sharpened, grew jagged, angry. Desperate.

There were no full names, no photos, just initials or pet names, often with small notes beside them:

> *"J. hated the restraints. Cried every time. Couldn't break her bad habits. Sent."*
>
> *"Elle. responded well. Grew too attached. Sent."*
>
> *"M3. said she loved me. Couldn't follow basic rules. Sent"*
>
> *"Sent. Sent. Sent."*

Sent. That word chilled me more than any punishment ever had. Sent *where?*

Each entry stacked on the last, a pattern emerging—one I didn't know what to do with. Some girls, she said, *Returned.* Did that mean they were allowed to leave? Maybe even *helped.* Others *Left.* Those entries were always followed by ink-smudged bitterness.

But *Sent…*

The most recent pages repeated it over and over.

> *"I gave her everything. She still broke rule six. Sent."*
>
> *"Screamed at me. Bit me. Sent."*
>
> *"Didn't even cry. Sent."*

My mouth went dry.

I shouldn't be reading this. Every page I turned made that truth louder. But I couldn't stop. I was already drowning in it, heart racing, skin prickled with goosebumps. This wasn't just control. It wasn't just dominance or kink or even trauma bonding.

This was a pattern. A cycle. And somehow, the newest name was mine. And if I wasn't careful... I might be the next one marked *Sent.*

The air felt thicker with each breath. I didn't know how long I'd been frozen there, crouched on the floor with the journal spread open like a confession.

I'd stopped turning pages, but not because I was done. I was stuck, unable to move, trying to process the weight of what I'd read. The word Sent burned in the back of my mind, over and over again.

A chill crawled down my spine before I even heard her voice.

"Find something interesting, pet?" her voice cooed from the doorway.

My blood turned to ice.

I jolted, the journal still open in my lap. Slowly, mechanically, I turned my head toward the doorway.

Domina stood there, leaning casually against the doorframe like she'd been there a while. Her arms were crossed beneath her chest, and a wicked smile curved her lips, one that didn't quite reach her eyes.

My mouth opened. Closed. Opened again. No sound came out. I snapped the journal shut with shaking hands and scrambled to my knees, the way I had been taught, eyes wide and pulse thundering

224

in my ears.

"I—I was just…" But there was no excuse that would make this better. No explanation that would undo what I'd seen, or what she had seen me doing.

"You were just…" she echoed softly, pushing off the door frame and walking into the room at an unhurried pace. "Snooping through something that doesn't belong to you?"

Her voice was calm. Even. *Too calm*. I couldn't breathe.

"I'm sorry," I whispered, my voice cracking as shame washed over me. "I just… I wanted to understand you."

Domina stopped in front of me. She crouched, meeting my eyes. Her smile faded, not into anger, but into something far more unsettling.

"I was going to *show you*," she said, her voice low, dangerous, almost tender. "I was going to *let* you know me, piece by piece. But now? Now I think we need to talk about *consequences*."

My heart pounded so loudly I could barely hear the words as she reached out, brushing a strand of hair behind my ear.

"And don't lie to me, pet. I want to know what you read. Every. Single. Word."

DOMINA

Chapter 36

Marianne stood, the cotton dress strap slipping down her shoulder as the blue color contrasted to her creamy freckled skin.

Her stance wasn't one of defiance, but not entirely with submission either.

Her hands were shaking, her brown eyes wide with fear and hurt, but she held herself upright, spine straight, chin trembling but lifted.

"I'm sorry," she said, the words hitting the air like a challenge and a plea in one breath. "I shouldn't have gone through your things... but I need to know."

I said nothing. I didn't move.

She took a breath, her voice cracking around the edges as she continued. "My name... it's not labeled. Yet. Not like the others." Her eyes searched my face, desperation flickering in them. "What happened to them? Why does it say *Left* or *Returned?* Or *Sent?*"

Sent. That one word stabbed through me like glass.

My jaw tightened. I could feel the muscles twitch.

She didn't know what she was asking. Or maybe she did, and that was worse.

I kept my expression still. I didn't trust my mouth to open without spilling everything I'd kept carefully, *methodically*, locked away. Her name wasn't labeled yet, no. Because I hadn't been able to bring myself to write it. Because I didn't know what it would be. *Because I didn't want her to become just another name in a list of failed endings.*

Marianne's brow furrowed. "What does Sent mean, Domina?"

I didn't answer.

She took a hesitant step forward, hands curling at her sides. "Did they ask to go? Did they… *not?*"

I wanted to scream. To tell her to *stop digging.* To *kneel.* To shut that beautiful, pleading mouth and let me hold the pieces of this in place just a little longer before it all shattered again.

But I didn't.

I let the silence stretch instead. I stared at her. And I let her feel every inch of that silence.

Because I didn't have an answer that didn't expose the crack inside me. The ugly truth.

Some were sent back because they begged to go. Some were sent because I couldn't let them stay. And some… some, I made vanish when they became dangerous.

And Marianne—*she was still deciding* what she would become.

I crossed my arms, the soft cotton of my button up comforting, grounding me in control.

"You're not ready for those answers, pet," I finally said, voice low, even, clipped.

Her shoulders dropped, and I saw it—*hurt*. Real hurt.

She didn't fall to her knees and I didn't tell her what *sent* really meant, because I didn't want to write it next to her name. Not ever.

Her expression crumpled for just a moment, just long enough for me to see the crack in her trust.

"I'm not ready?" she repeated, voice rising slightly, incredulous. "After everything we've done! Everything I've *given you* and you still get to decide what I'm ready for?"

I straightened, every muscle in my spine going taut. "*Yes*, pet," I said, tone flat. Cold. "Because this—" I gestured loosely between us, between the desk and the open journal, "—was not part of your permission. You broke my trust."

Her eyes welled, but she didn't back down. "I'm *not* just another one of them. Am I? Am I just another name you write down when you're done?"

That landed like a slap. But I didn't flinch. I wouldn't give her that. I could see she wanted to be special. To be more.

She was trembling now, but her voice was steadier than I expected. "Why is my name not labeled yet, Domina? Because you haven't decided whether you're going to send me or break me?"

"Watch your mouth," I snapped, sharper than I intended.

The silence that followed that command was so heavy it pressed on my chest.

I had crossed lines with the others, blurred things. Bent the rules. Always in the name of finding the right one. The one who could match my darkness without flinching. The one who *wouldn't* leave me. The one I didn't have to destroy or release.

They always left. Or I made them leave before they could choose to.

She stood before me—my *pet*, my *weakness*, my undoing in bare feet and raw emotion—holding that fucking journal like it held the truth about *me* inside of it.

I stepped forward, just once, slow and deliberate, until she tilted her chin up defiantly to meet my eyes.

"I haven't labeled you," I said, voice quiet now, but razor sharp. "Because I don't know what the fuck you are yet."

Her face froze.

"You think that journal is full of answers? It's a graveyard," I hissed. "Of failures. Of mistakes. Of subs who couldn't handle what they *begged me* for. I gave them everything. I carved space in myself for them. And when it got too *real*, too *deep*, they ran."

I saw the way she recoiled, just a flinch, but I saw it. Good. I needed her to feel it. To understand that this wasn't a fairytale. That I wasn't a safe place.

"I didn't *send* them," I whispered darkly, stepping even closer. "They *chose*. Or they broke. And when they did, I protected what I had left."

I didn't explain what that meant. I wouldn't. She didn't get to see that part of me. Not until I was sure.

She was quiet now. Breathing hard. Eyes locked on mine like she was trying to decide whether to bolt or kneel.

"Tell me right now," I said, voice barely a breath. "Are you still mine?"

She hesitated.

Fuck, I was already preparing myself to let her go if she said no.

Chapter 37

I didn't say anything. How could I? I didn't even really know her.

The weight of her stare lingered in the room even after she walked away. I stood there gripping the edge of the desk like it could anchor me. My stomach churned with something more than guilt. It was fear. Not the sharp, frantic kind, but something slow and suffocating, like thick fog filling my lungs.

I shouldn't have opened that book. I knew that. But knowing didn't erase the part of me that wanted—no, needed—to know. I wanted to understand the kind of woman I had given myself to, piece by trembling piece.

What did "Sent" mean?

What had happened to the others?

Why hadn't she labeled me yet?

The journal said too much and not enough. Domina had secrets, and I had willingly walked into her web, baring myself, letting her bind me with her touch, her rules, her voice. Things had changed, I didn't know if I was safe or shackled. Did those words even mean the same thing to me anymore?

I couldn't deny it, I wanted to trust her. I wanted to believe that what we had and what we were building was more than just another name in her ledger. Maybe I was different. That maybe I could be enough.

Still… Could I handle the answers? Could I handle whatever came next?

I leaned back against the desk and waited, my breath grew shallow, my heart louder than reason.

No matter how hard the truth landed in my gut. If she asked me to beg, I knew I would. If she asked me to kneel, I already had. God help me, I was hers, in every fucking way.

The door opened again, this time with purpose.

Domina stepped inside, quiet as ever, but something had changed in her. Her movements were deliberate, almost sharp with an edge I hadn't felt since the first time she made me beg. In her hands, she held a long, black velvet box. It looked heavy with meaning.

She didn't speak as she crossed the room. She just held my gaze and set the box in my hands with a kind of reverence that made my fingers tremble around the edges.

I looked up at her, expecting fury. Though, her face was unreadable, calm. Too calm. It was the kind of silence that came just before a storm.

She stepped back, arms behind her back like she was bracing herself, and then she said it.

"Are you mine, pet?" Her voice was low but commanding. "And will you be, from now until death?"

The words hung in the air, more binding than any collar, any contract. I froze. The weight of the box in my lap felt heavier now, like a final choice. My pulse thundered in my ears.

I wanted to ask what was inside. I wanted to ask what she meant by death. I wanted to ask about the other girls, what it meant to be Sent, or Left. I wanted answers, and I wanted time.

But she was offering no time. Only now. Only everything.

Was I hers? God. I already was.

The question wasn't if she had me. It was as if I was ready to admit it out loud.

My lips parted. My voice cracked. But the truth was already blooming inside my chest, tangled with fear and something dangerously close to devotion.

"Domina," I whispered, breathless. "I...."

The velvet of the box burned against my palms.

"Then open it," she said softly.

My fingers trembled as I unfastened the soft clasp holding the box shut. The velvet creaked faintly under my touch as I opened the lid, revealing what lay inside.

A collar.

Oxblood red, deep and rich and impossible to mistake. The leather was smooth and thick, polished to a near shine. A single gold ring gleamed at the front, flanked by two smaller ones on either side. The buckle was heavy and gold as well—practical, elegant, and utterly final.

But it was the nameplate that stole my breath.

Mari.

Etched in bold letters. Clean. Permanent.

Not Marianne. Not pet. Not girl.

Mari.

My name, but hers now too, reclaimed, reshaped, reborn under her ownership.

My throat clenched, emotion hitting me so hard I had to blink rapidly to keep from crying. No one had ever seen me like this. No one had ever wanted to mark me with such terrifying tenderness.

My fingers brushed the plate, then hovered just above the thick band of leather.

"I had it made the week after you sent your first photo," Domina said quietly from across the room. "I didn't know why then. I just... knew."

Her voice broke slightly, and when I looked up, I saw the smallest crack in her mask—her fear, her longing, her want of me.

She stepped forward and her fingers glided along the collar. "So are you mine, Mari?"

Epilogue – Jenny

A few nights earlier…

The blue light of my phone bathed the sheets in a sterile glow, the kind you find in morgues or hospital rooms just before a flatline. I scrolled up, rereading the last message.

S.Auction

Do you have another one to sell me yet? I've got a buyer requesting your work by name. They'll pay double.

My thumb hovered above the keyboard. My chest rose and fell slowly, not with nerves—but with the familiar thrill of control, of choice. I typed the response without blinking.

Me

Not yet. This one… she's special. I'm keeping her. Tell them two months. I'll start prepping the next one.

I stared at the blinking cursor for a moment, then pressed send.

Beside me, Marianne shifted in her sleep, murmuring something soft, sweet, and completely unaware. I turned toward her and slipped an arm around her bare waist, pulling her close, breathing her in. She nestled against me like I was home. Like I wasn't the monster.

I brushed my lips across her temple.

She didn't stir.

She never would—until I let her.

Content Warning / Trigger List:

This book contains graphic and potentially distressing content, including:

Abduction / Kidnapping (central to the plot)
Dubious Consent / Non-consensual elements
Power Imbalance & Psychological Manipulation
BDSM Dynamics including:
Spanking, caning, belting,
Orgasm control & denial
Bondage & restraint,
Electro-stimulation
Degradation, humiliation, & punishment
Ownership dynamics, collaring, and behavioral protocols Religious Trauma and internalized shame
Mentions of arranged marriage / forced heterosexual norms
Emotional dependency / trauma bonding themes
Explicit Sexual Content including oral, penetrative, and kink-focused scenes
Mentions of past relationships with implied coercion or abandonment
Implied sex trafficking (in the epilogue / backstory context)
Manipulation disguised as care and emotional intimacy

This story contains intense emotional dynamics, dark eroticism, and explores unhealthy behavior patterns within a fictional context. Reader discretion is strongly advised.

This is intended for 18+ audiences only.

Your Mental Health Matters

For anyone struggling with mental health
or feeling unsafe:
Mental Health Crisis Hotline (U.S.)
📞 988 (Call or Text)
Get connected to free, confidential support anytime.
You are not alone. Help exists—and hope does too.

From Fiction to Fact

While *Twisted in the Darkness* is a work of fiction, the
themes within—coercion, captivity, manipulation, and
power imbalance—reflect real horrors experienced by
victims of human trafficking.

Human trafficking is a global crisis that affects millions. It
does not always look like chains or locked doors.
It can look like manipulation, grooming, false promises,
and control masked as love.
If you or someone you know is being trafficked
—or you suspect it—
please contact:
National Human Trafficking Hotline (U.S.)
📞 1-888-373-7888 (24/7 confidential support)
📱 Text "BEFREE" (233733)
🌐 humantraffickinghotline.org
Your call could save a life.
Your voice could break a chain.

Coercion Isn't Faith

When belief becomes control, it's no longer sacred. Religious extremism, cultic manipulation, and spiritual abuse can leave lasting emotional, psychological, and physical scars. If you've been part of a high-control religious group or know someone who might be, you're not alone—and there is help.

Recognizing Religious Coercion:

- Are questions met with punishment or shame?
- Is isolation from family or the outside world encouraged?
- Do you feel fear, guilt, or unworthiness unless you comply?
- Are your choices, body, or future dictated by a leader or doctrine?
-

These are not signs of healthy spiritual practice.

Support & Recovery Resources:

International Cultic Studies Association (ICSA)
For survivors, families, and professionals seeking information or recovery support
🌐 icsahome.com

People Leave Cults
Offering outreach, exit counseling, and survivor-informed support
🌐 peopleleavecults.com

Reclamation Collective
Faith deconstruction and trauma-informed healing community
🌐 reclamationcollective.com

Acknowledgements

To my incredible BookTok community - your enthusiasm, support, and chaos have made this journey unforgettable. Thank you for championing this story from whispers of an idea to a finished book in your hands. You remind me daily why I keep writing.

To my alpha readers - who saw the raw bones first and still came back for more. Thank you for your honesty and hype.

To my beta readers - thank you for diving deep and helping shape the heart of this book. Your feedback has been a guiding light.

And to every ARC reader - who took a chance on an early copy and helped spread the word. I am endlessly grateful.

A special and resounding thank you to Leslie Swartz, my editor and literary backbone. Your insights, patience, and precision helped me bring clarity to chaos and make every dark corner shine a little brighter.

This book wouldn't exist without all of you. Thank you for believing in me.

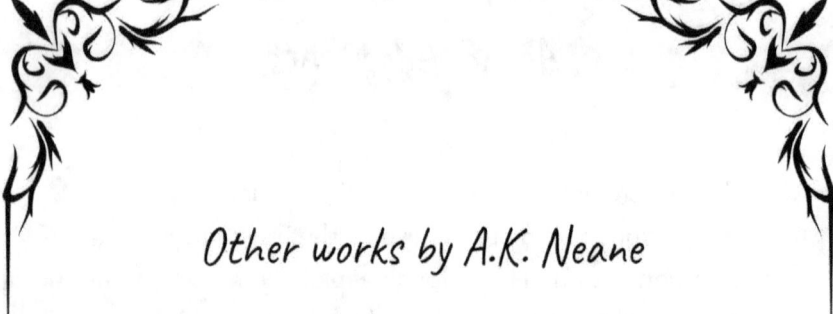

Other works by A.K. Neane

Veins of Sapphire,
Hearts of Steel

Shadows of the Ironwilde -
Coming Sept. 2026

About the Author

A.K. Neane (they/them) is a queer fantasy author who believes in the power of storytelling to create safe spaces and amplify diverse voices. Inspired by the comfort books have always provided, they craft immersive worlds filled with magic, complex characters, and the kind of representation they longed for growing up.

When not writing, they can be found wrangling their teens or goats on their small family farm, researching mythology, or diving into their next obsession.

Veins of Sapphire, Hearts of Steel is their debut novel, the first in the Destiny of Terraqua trilogy.

Stay connected for updates, exclusive content, and behind-the-scenes insights:

@A.K.Neane.Author

www.ingramcontent.com/pod-product-compliance
Lightning Source LLC
Chambersburg PA
CBHW060314260626
47160CB00007B/2607